2009 Content

KT-116-540

p108

p152

Poppy's Prize

by Joanne Ford.

A RE we nearly there yet?"
Luke's voice was at that
awkward stage of breaking, as
though he had laryngitis.

Poppy kept her finger riveted to the dot
on the map.

"Not much farther," she replied, as she'd
done when the children were little. Now
they'd shot up into a pair of restless
teenagers, still asking the same question.

"You said that hours ago," husband Matt
groaned from the driver's seat.

"But look at the beautiful scenery," Poppy
urged, willing her family to share her
enthusiasm. "Look at those hills. And that's the
sea."

She pointed to the grey line on the horizon, realising too
late that she'd lost the dot. She bent her head to find it again,
her erratic blonde curls falling across her face.

"I'm cold," Sasha grumbled behind her, in a cocoon of black sweaters and
scarves. "How can going to the seaside in December be a sensible idea?"

"Oh, Sasha, we've been over this."

Poppy turned to peer at her children through the gap between the headrests.
Luke, at fourteen, was fair-haired like her. Sasha, one year younger, was dark
like Matt.

Poppy used to congratulate herself on having such a neatly arranged family.
But nowadays they seemed to disagree with her at every opportunity.

"Do you know how much it would cost to hire this cottage for a week at
New Year? Hundreds. And we won it for free, courtesy of the Tourist Board."
Poppy gave them a bright smile, her blue eyes radiating delight. "Aren't we
lucky?"

Luke and Sasha exchanged a dubious glance. Poppy returned to the map,
refusing to be discouraged. The trouble with her family was that they

Illustration by
Adam Hook.

sometimes needed pointing
in the direction of enjoyment.

This holiday was to be the perfect
solution to that post-Christmas lull. Usually she'd be sitting at home, thinking
of the extra pounds she'd gained, and wondering whether it was worthwhile
making such an effort to organise Christmas. For once she could leave that
behind. And how many more New Years would they spend together? Soon
the children would be going off to parties with their friends. They should
make the most of this time. Once they got into the holiday mood they'd have
a fantastic week — Poppy was convinced of it.

✳   ✳   ✳   ✳

They wound their way along a sandy lane and finally came to a squat blue
bungalow at the far end of the beach road. The sign above the door said
Seaview Cottage and, as promised, a key lay hidden beneath a plant pot.
Poppy dashed inside, unable to contain her excitement.

The place was more modern than she'd expected. Vintage 1980s in fact. But it was clean, comfortable and, most importantly, the radiators were hot.

"Isn't it wonderful?" she called as the others came in. "Sort out which room you want and I'll unpack the food."

Matt followed her into the kitchen.

"Correct me if I'm wrong, but didn't you say you'd won a luxury cottage? How does that translate to a small bungalow?"

Poppy waved her hand, trying to bat the question away.

"Oh, I do so many competitions. I don't remember exactly what it said now. It was a prize draw in one of those holiday brochures."

"You and your prizes." He had a naturally serious face, but his voice was warm with mild amusement.

"Something about this situation reminds me of that picnic hamper you won. We had to go on a trip to the lake especially so we could use it and got bitten half to death by horseflies."

"Oh, Matt! This is nothing like the picnic hamper."

THE way he teased her about the competitions anyone would think she always won white elephants. Poppy had only started doing them in the first place because Matt was made redundant. The children needed so many things and she'd had to be resourceful. A streak of good fortune had brought a Wendy house for Sasha, a football kit for Luke.

Matt had found another job, but by then the competitions had become something of an addiction.

"Anyway, it's fun winning things, isn't it?" she said, trying to cajole him into a smile. "You never know what's going to arrive next."

"Like the set of cast iron saucepans that were too heavy for the shelf?" he said with the ghost of a twinkle in his eye. "It took me a weekend to retile the wall."

Poppy giggled.

"Yes, but they were a gorgeous colour."

"I just hope the house won't freeze up while we're away."

"The house will be fine. Relax. The heating's on low and your sister's going round every day to feed the fish."

Honestly, Poppy thought. Did he expect the house might be swept up by a whirlwind, like in "The Wizard Of Oz"?

She looked at her husband as he leant against the sink. He was tall, angular, with a tendency to worry. Poppy thought it was just as well that she was blessed with boundless optimism. She had enough for the two of them.

"This holiday was a great chance to celebrate New Year somewhere different. You know how important it is to me that we do things as a family," she added, giving him her slightly lost look which always won him over.

Poppy was only eight when her parents divorced. Afterwards there was for ever someone missing. If she was with her mum, her dad wasn't there. If she was with her dad, her mum wasn't there. The aunts, uncles, cousins and grandparents had divided themselves up according to their loyalties. From then on the one thing she'd wanted was to have a proper family again, with everyone together in the same place. Was that too much to ask?

"I know," Matt said, crossing the room to rest his hands on her shoulders. "But don't forget, we came on one condition."

If the cottage was horrible, the children were bored or the weather was awful they'd go home on New Year's Day. That was the promise Poppy had made. But she was sure it wouldn't come to that. This holiday would be really special — one they'd always remember. She had no doubts about it.

S O, tomorrow will be New Year's Eve," she said later, as they sat eating spaghetti around the breakfast bar. "We can go out somewhere in the daytime. Maybe walk along the coastal path."

Sasha twirled spaghetti on to her fork and looked thoughtful.

"Is there, like, a town? With shops? There might be some sales on."

"Shame your mother didn't win you a chauffeur," Matt retorted.

"I'll drive," Poppy volunteered. "The town's only ten miles away."

"I want to spend my Christmas money on a new computer game," Luke broke in. "Will there be anywhere we can get on to the internet?"

Poppy pursed her lips.

"Well, I'm not sure if it's that big a town. But we'll have a good look. We can treat ourselves to a nice lunch out. And then in the evening we'll hold our own private party. Won't that be lovely?"

*   *   *   *

When Poppy woke next morning Matt was still snoring beside her and the house was quiet. She rolled on to her back and stared at the ceiling. What would the New Year bring? Would Luke start dating girls and find a band to play his guitar with? Would Sasha persist in her plan to become a teacher and work abroad? Slowly but surely, they were growing away from her. Just a little longer, that was all she wanted. A little more time of having them with her, sharing adventures. Trying to give them what she had missed as a child

— a sense of belonging.

And what about her and Matt? Perhaps she should increase her hours at the hospital now the children were growing up. Maybe Matt could set up his own business, as he'd always wanted.

What a terrific way to see in 2009, staying by the sea in their windfall of a cottage. She couldn't stay in bed another minute. Carefully, she eased herself out and peeked through the curtains. She gasped in horror. No! It couldn't be . . .

Huge snowflakes fell from the dark sky. Poppy couldn't tell how bad it was, but the ground looked white all over.

"Wassup?" Matt mumbled from the bed.

"Nothing." She closed the curtain quickly. "Go back to sleep."

Wrapped in her lilac dressing-gown, she padded to the kitchen. The view from there was just as white. And from the lounge it was worse, since she could make out the blurred shape of their car swathed in snow. She leaned her forehead against the cold window-pane.

Now the others would have a field day. She'd dragged them all this distance to be snowed in.

Matt would mope around the bungalow, fretting about the house and the fish. Sasha hated the cold. Poppy put it down to being born during a July heatwave. She'd take one look outside and insist on staying in bed with a book. And Luke needed constant entertainment otherwise he'd get tetchy and pick on his sister.

This was terrible.

GRADUALLY the sky turned to violet-grey, then to milky-white while Poppy sat drinking tea at the breakfast bar. The snow was falling so fast she couldn't even see the hill behind the bungalow. Matt drifted in and looked at the snowy scene on the patio. He drew a deep breath and blew it out again as if he was extinguishing a candle.

"Guess we won't be needing that barbecue."

Sasha arrived wearing her black kimono with the dragon on the back.

"What time are we going?" she asked, bleary-eyed.

"You know, we might have to put off that trip to town," Poppy answered as gently as she could.

Then Luke wandered in, his hair sticking up from not yet having encountered a comb.

"What? We're staying here all day?"

Poppy bit her lip and looked at each of them.

"No sales?" Sasha asked.

"No internet?" Luke moaned.

"But you said the town wasn't far," Sasha said accusingly. She sank on to a stool at the breakfast bar with her head in her hands as though this was the

Step Back In Time

The Old Age Pensions Act

ONE hundred years ago, on January 1, 1909, the Liberal government's Old Age Pensions Act came into force.

At the turn of the century, the Liberal government's policy of *laissez-faire* meant that it was not the responsibility of the government to intervene in the life of an individual — therefore, any problems or hardship you encountered were seen as your own fault and responsibility.

However, as a new century dawned, the Liberal government was facing increasing pressure to provide help for those in need.

Two separate surveys into poverty by businessmen Charles Booth and Seebohm Rowntree revealed that up to thirty per cent of urban populations were living below the poverty line.

Many were so very poor that it would have been impossible for them to deal with the problem themselves.

These surveys also pinpointed the main causes of poverty — illness, unemployment and age. It soon became clear that, in order to combat poverty, the roots of the problem would have to be addressed.

Liberals David Lloyd George and Winston Churchill.

PA.

Aside from proving that poverty had causes that were out of the control of the individual, the reports also indicated that it was a widespread problem.

Booth's initial survey took place in London where it was known there was a great degree of poverty. Rowntree's survey, however, took place in York — a town that was considered to be affluent.

The Liberals introduced a number of reforms to protect the vulnerable of society. The National Insurance Act and the Children's Charter were brought in to help protect the workers and the young.

In order to protect the elderly, the Old Age Pensions Act, 1908, was first introduced.

It gave a single person over the age of seventy five shillings a week. Married couples over seventy received slightly more, and higher earners, slightly less.

However, not everyone received the pension — if you were deemed to be of "bad character", had habitually avoided work or had been in prison, you were exempt from the scheme.

Although the Old Age Pensions Act was set out to help the most vulnerable members of society, it still met with some criticism.

Firstly, the Act was not deemed to go far enough. The amount of money received was a pittance and barely supplemented an existing income, let alone pay solely for living costs.

Also, many elderly people needed help before reaching pensionable age. As Booth and Rowntree had proven, poverty was deep-rooted in society and many had fallen below the poverty line long before they reached seventy — an impressive age to reach a hundred years ago. Few lived to see their seventieth year, let alone their pension.

However, those who did receive their pension on January 1, 1909 were ecstatic and extremely grateful to the government. From post offices across the land, where the pensions could be collected, tears of joy were shed and cries of thanks to David Lloyd George rang out across the winter skies. ■

worst thing to have happened in her thirteen years. "This holiday is as much use as that coffee-maker you won."

The one time Poppy had used the espresso machine, the coffee was so strong she'd felt jittery the rest of the day from the caffeine. Now it took up a chunk of her worktop like a shiny instrument from a science lab.

"Yeah," Luke joined in. "Why do you do these competitions, Mum? What about the year's supply of cat food you won last Christmas?"

"The animal rescue centre was grateful," Poppy said. "And Sasha loved her Wendy house."

"Mum — I was six!" Sasha cried, throwing her hands into the air.

Luke paced around as though he was already feeling claustrophobic.

"We can't stay indoors all day. There must be somewhere we can go."

Poppy looked at Matt, but he didn't seem inclined to bail her out.

"I don't think we could get the car down the road," she said sadly. "Look — there's even snow on the beach."

"Snow on the beach?" Luke echoed. He shook his head. "No way. That's impossible."

"It's true. See for yourself." She went to stand beside him at the window.

Luke studied the narrow strip of sand separating the waves from the snow.

"That's weird. That's the weirdest thing I ever saw. Come and look, Sash."

Poppy saw the remotest glimmer of a chance to salvage the day.

"I bet none of your friends are beside a beach covered in snow."

"Cool!" Luke exclaimed. "Let's get down there and take some pictures."

Poppy felt the tension lessen slightly in the room. That was her son all right, nought to sixty in ten seconds flat.

Sasha stared at them as though they were crazy.

"But it's freezing. We can't seriously go to the beach. We'll get pneumonia. Or frostbite. Or disappear in a snowdrift."

Matt sat down next to her, giving her a quick nudge with his elbow.

"Do it for your mother."

Although there were times when Matt drove Poppy to distraction with his cautious approach to the world, in that moment she remembered why she'd married him.

AN hour later, bundled up like Eskimos against the cold, Luke and Sasha took turns to photograph each other on their mobile phones and send the pictures to their friends. The snow had stopped falling and the sky was turning to the palest blue. Waves broke a few feet away, the sound oddly muffled.

Inevitably, Luke scooped up a handful of snow and hurled it at his sister. Sasha retaliated and soon all four of them were involved in a snowball fight. Poppy shrieked as snow went down the back of her neck and Matt laughed in a way she hadn't seen him laugh for months.

"You know, with this weather we might not be able to get home tomorrow," Poppy said to him as they walked along the beach, following footprints made by the children racing on ahead.

"The thought had occurred to me," he replied, putting an arm around her. "Not that you wanted to go home tomorrow."

"No, but I would have if the kids were fed up."

She felt a sudden rush of longing, watching the children stride up the beach. For a moment she thought of the holidays they'd had when they were small. All the snapshots of the caravans, boat trips and picnics. Luke had always been impetuous, Sasha always solemn. But at least back then she could jolly them along.

Now they weren't children any more. Young adults, really, with their own lives and independent minds. Sometimes she had this sense of them veering off from her, when she wanted to keep them anchored down to the family. She'd have to start letting go, sooner rather than later.

"I know they'd probably rather be with their friends back home," she admitted. "And I know this holiday's gone a bit haywire. But we're having fun, aren't we?"

"I guess things do have a habit of becoming fun when you're around."

"Oh, Matt," she said, giving him an affectionate poke in the ribs. "I so wanted us to have a New Year to remember."

"I'm pretty sure we'll remember it."

They caught up with the children at the top of the beach and the four of them turned to walk back together.

"Hey, Dad," Luke said. "Me and Sash decided you should make a New Year's resolution to give us more pocket money."

"Well, maybe you should resolve to get a paper round," Matt countered swiftly.

"I think Sasha should resolve to wear colours other than black," Poppy suggested.

"And we know what you should do, Mum," Sasha said. "Give up competitions."

Luke and Matt both laughed in agreement. Poppy laughed, too, just to be part of the joke. Give up competitions? Hardly. She'd saved a dozen soap wrappers towards winning a swimming pool.

A glow of happiness replaced the feeling of loss. It could take days for the roads to clear. They'd muddle through as a family, like they always did.

Tomorrow the kids would sleep late, having stayed up past midnight. Perhaps there would be a pub close by where they could go for a meal. There was a cupboard of old games at the bungalow.

And then the next day . . . Oh, why bother about the next day? Tonight she'd have her family around her as midnight struck and a new year began. And Poppy couldn't wish for any better prize than that. ■

I'M standing at the door, fascinated, as I watch my little Amy carefully build a snowman. She's such a perfectionist — just like her daddy really — and everything has to be just so . . .

I see her deftly scoop and pile crisp white snow with hands that are encased in soggy, red woollen mittens. Inch by freezing inch, she sculpts the rounded figure of a snowman in the last of the afternoon light.

Her little brother, Jake, never one to be left out or to take his time at anything — he's more like me — bombs around the garden looking for the finishing touches to Mr Frosty.

I should be really happy, watching my children enjoy simple childish fun in this, the first snow of winter. Yet today I'm struggling to hold back the tears as I can't help thinking that this may well be the last snowman I'll see them build. That sobering thought fills me with a sadness as cold as the day itself.

I know it's too late to change my mind. I've let it go too far, and we did make our choice together.

by Hilary Halliwell.

This life-changing move we're about to undertake fills me with trepidation, but it will work out for the best, or at least that's what I keep telling myself.

"Mummy!" A very red, very cold and very wet Jake jumps up and down in front of me. "Have you got any black buttons for Mr Frosty's coat? And a hat, he has to have a hat, and a scarf. You always make us wear a scarf, don't you, Mummy?"

He's so excited, he's practically breathless.

"What about a carrot for his nose?" Amy chips in, and I smile genuinely for the first time that day.

Illustration by Kiri Hardy.

JAKE goes to follow me into the house and I have to grab him to stop him running over the carpet.

"Take your boots off first, young man. You're going nowhere with

14

those snow-covered boots on!"

We finally make it through to the kitchen and I get my granny's button jar out of the Welsh dresser. Tipping it out on to the dining table, I smile to myself as freezing little fingers search for the perfect four buttons for Mr Frosty's coat.

I recognise buttons from years ago — the children's ones, my dad's ones and my own. There must be hundreds of buttons in the jar.

"Can we have these ones, please, Mummy?"

Jake picks out four shiny, black domed buttons that I remember from my granny's winter coat a million years or so ago. I'm so glad I kept her button jar; she'd be delighted that they came in handy for Jake and Amy. It's such a shame that she never got the chance to meet them.

Snowman

I dig out a long, pointy carrot from my veg box and then collect my dad's old red scarf from the umbrella stand in the hall. He left it behind one winter and never bothered to take it away, always joking that it might come in handy one day when he's forgotten where he left his current one.

THEN I take an old baseball cap from a hook in the understairs cupboard.

"Here we are, everything old Frosty-pants needs!" I say, handing the items to Jake, and he shrieks with laughter at my rechristening of the snowman.

"Thanks, Mum. You won't come out and look till we've finished, will you?" he asks with furrowed little brow. And he's gone out the door like a mini-tornado, closely followed by Mutley,

15

our dog, who's been woken from his afternoon nap by all the noise.

"Only thirty minutes more and then you're both in, Jake. It'll be dark soon. Jake, did you hear me?"

But it's too late, the door has slammed behind him and I'm left with my doubts and fears about what we are about to do.

I grew up in this sleepy little town of Christchurch. I went to school here, the same school that my two children go to now. I played on the same swings at the same recreation ground, and probably bought my ice-cream from the same tatty van that came down our street every afternoon, chimes blaring, just like it does even now.

I had my first date here, courted my Mike here and our children were christened in the same church where we were married. Why on earth would we leave? We must be mad.

Christchurch is a lovely place to live. The sea is just a stone's throw from our house and the forest practically sits on our doorstep. So why, oh, why, are we going to the other side of the world and leaving all this behind?

WE'D been to visit Mike's older brother, Nigel, and his lovely wife, Anna, before the children were born. It had been a wonderful holiday, and the last we would be able to afford before starting to save for a bigger house.

Australia is a truly beautiful and diverse country, and especially so on the Gold Coast where they live. It was, and still is, a land full of opportunity, and Nigel and Anna had fired our enthusiasm for a share of the good life. Not to mention the sun-kissed beaches and houses with more room than we'd ever be able to afford here in Great Britain.

"Come on, Mike," Nigel had enthused. "With two of us working together, there isn't anything we couldn't achieve. They're crying out for plumbers over here. We could start our own business!"

"Oh, Juliet, it'd be great — our kids would grow up together. We'd be best mates as well as family," Anna had said warmly.

Anna's a lovely girl. I can see why Nigel followed her back to her native land. They met when she was over in Britain on a gap year and he'd been smitten. The whole family had been sad to see him go, but it was wonderful to see him so happy and so in love . . .

We'd taken a month's holiday there. Three weeks with Nigel and Anna and their new baby, Benny. Then we'd had a week in Sydney, just the two of us, on a romantic belated honeymoon.

It'd been the holiday of a lifetime, but to go and live there? Move away from quaint little Christchurch? Leave my mum and dad and my family? I wasn't sure even then that I could do it.

After we returned home to England we had talked on and off for several years about the possibility of a new life in Australia. Not that I ever really thought it would happen. It was only after the children were born that it suddenly became a reality and last summer we made the final decision to emigrate.

We put the house on the market, were still considering two offers, and Mike got a job with the same plumbing firm in Australia that Nigel works for.

Mike's parents had been very philosophical about our decision to leave. I thought they were very brave considering Nigel was in Australia already. It can't have been too easy for them to think of all their family on the other side of the world.

My mum had tried her hardest to be positive, but I could see right through her.

"It's not that far away these days, pet. Besides, it'll give your dad and me somewhere to go for our holidays. And you'll be able to come home and visit, won't you? You've got to do what's right for your family and we're only a phone call away."

Mum had said all the right things, but I could tell that she was shocked by our decision, no matter how hard she tried to convince me otherwise.

My dad had been less enthusiastic, but he had come round in the end. I think my mum had had a word with him and, although he was sad, he managed to put on a brave face.

THAT was all four short months ago. I say short because time's flown by and now here we are, on the crest of a wave that will take us to the other side of the globe. Perhaps that's why I'm having such major last minute doubts. Why had I ever agreed to it?

And now, as I stand by the kettle in the kitchen of my cosy little house, I can think of nothing but the simple pleasures of family and snowmen and memories — all centred here in beautiful Dorset where we belong.

I walk over to the window and look out at my two frozen children. Mr Frosty is looking spectacular and I congratulate myself on what talented children I have!

"Mummy, come and see him," Amy calls, her bright blue eyes and smile lighting not only her pretty face but the gloom of my mood.

"He's wonderful," I tell my two snow-covered angels with a proud smile, standing in the doorway with a cup of hot coffee.

"Mum, look, he's finished. We don't have to come in yet, do we?" Jake asks, ever the optimist.

"Yes, I'm afraid so! Mr Frosty will still be there in the morning."

By the time they get boots off, mittens on the radiators and snowsuits hung up in the hall cupboard, my coffee is cold, but it doesn't matter as we all go through to the kitchen and sit down together at the table for hot chocolate to warm us up.

Mutley is steaming himself dry from his romp in the snow as he snoozes before the fire. We've had him for two years now, ever since he came to us from the rescue centre, and Mum and Dad are taking him on when we leave for Oz. Dad says he'll be good exercise and Mutley loves my dad, but I will miss him, just like I'll miss all of this.

The children will miss him terribly, too. Mutley is part of the family now and just one more poignant reminder today of what we're leaving behind.

How can I go through with this? My heart is breaking just thinking about it.

The front door opening says Mike is home from work at last. I'll talk to him tonight, after the children are in bed. I'll tell him how I feel. I just hope he'll understand. Surely he will? I love him so much and I wouldn't want anything to come between us now.

✳   ✳   ✳   ✳

I'm sitting here watching Amy building a sandcastle whilst Jake and Benny tear about the beach looking for shells and twigs to decorate the wonky towers and turrets.

And no — we didn't up sticks and move to the other side of the world last year after all! I spoke to Mike that night, the night I thought I'd seen our children build the last snowman. I told him how I really felt, told him that, even though it was a little house that we lived in, it was home.

I explained that, no matter how grand, no matter what the opportunities or rewards on offer, what could ever hold a candle to what we have here, nestled in the bosom of our family? Dorset, with its unreliable summer weather and its snowmen, along with its memories, would be irreplaceable.

I have to confess that I was nervous. After all, we had talked all of this out, and I was the one who was now going back on our plans.

But do you know what? I needn't have worried about Mike because it turned out he felt just the same. He'd just wanted to give us a better life, but what could be better than to stay where your heart is?

SO, you see, Mr Frosty wasn't the last snowman after all. In fact, just a few months ago, our new little daughter, Bethany, watched from her daddy's arms as Jake, Amy, Mutley and me, of course, put those same black buttons from Granny's button jar on a brand new Mr Frosty.

He's here on the photos that I sit showing to my sister-in-law, Anna. They've come over for a holiday and it's so good to see them again. They're even enjoying the great British weather — with its changeable days. Seemingly, when you're used to constant sunshine and heat, cloudy days can be paradise!

We're all here enjoying the day — Mike and me, our parents, Anna, Nigel, Benny, and not forgetting our three darlings — or Mutley, of course.

He's getting on a bit, but still enjoys a trip to the beach every now and again. Yes, we're all together again in our very own little bit of paradise — here on the beach at Christchurch. ∎

ANNIE pushed hard to open the door of the dirty railway carriage and looked anxiously at the crowd on the platform. There was no sight of a porter, but Harold was there, waiting for her.

He was hovering about, peering into the grimy train windows and then looking back at the open doors — obviously anxious for his first sight of her. His height gave him an advantage over those waiting on the platform for their relations or waiting to get on to the train to go to Leigh.

"Coo-ee! Harry! I'm over here," she called, waving her hand in the air frantically. He spotted her at once and rushed towards her, a wide grin lighting up his face.

I might have known — just look at the state of him, Annie thought. Harold hadn't even bothered to get himself changed and was standing in front of her in his working man's uniform — flat cap, white silk scarf tied loosely up and over round his neck, greyish-white shirt and grubby old suit jacket.

His ill-fitting trousers were held up

Forget Me Not

by Sheila Culshaw.

Illustration by
Andy Walker.

19

by the broad belt the miners always wore to support their backs when working down the pit.

She tossed her hair and raised her eyes heavenwards in despair.

"Just look at the state of you, Harold Calderbank. This is supposed to be a special occasion. It's been three whole months since I last saw you," she said, teasing him a little. "I can see you'll need a good sorting out when we get wed."

"Well, you're just the one to do that," Harold said boldly, and smiled his quiet, confident smile at her from under the brim of his cap. His dark eyes were warm, full of affection, and Annie revelled in the fact that his affection was reserved just for her. He'd said he'd loved her when he was sixteen and had never changed his mind. Now, finally, she'd decided she was ready to be his wife and had come back home from the estate where she had been working as a house servant.

"Oh, Harold, I am glad to see you."

"Me, too." That was enough for the moment. Their faces said the rest.

"I can't manage my big case by myself, Harold. It's in the guard's van. Would you mind getting it for me?" she asked, and Harold rushed off.

WELL, here I am, back home again — back where I started from, and this time for good, Annie thought, looking round at the dirty brick station wall. She sighed. This was where she belonged. Her relations all lived in this town, but she was a determined girl who'd wanted to see life before she'd married, and had gone into service when she was sixteen. The master of the house she had worked in owned the pit where Harold worked. Now she'd come back permanently, although she had visited her home and Harold every time she had a holiday . . .

She was wearing her best coat and skirt and her smart velveteen "church" hat to impress Harold, and was carrying a small cardboard suitcase in her gloved hands. She looked down at her new gloves, admiring them, and picked at a stitch while she waited for Harold.

Then she saw him again, a short distance away. He was showing off his strength and swinging the big suitcase as if it was no weight at all.

"Is there owt else, love?"

"No, that's it."

The air smelled of a mixture of coal dust and smoke — smoke from the engine of the train, smoke from the pits. There was dust in the air and dust up her nostrils. Her face felt dirty. Annie sneezed and took a clean handkerchief from her pocket.

"I don't know how you manage to carry that suitcase, it's a ton weight," she said admiringly as Harry strode up the hill, swaggering along with his workman's confident stride. Annie trotted along beside him in her Sunday best boots, and suddenly she felt shy, and unable to think of anything to say.

Harold stopped at a lamp-post and dropped the enormous suitcase on the flags while he tried manfully to get his breath back.

"'My word," he said, rubbing a chafed, calloused hand. Obviously carrying the suitcase had been hard work. "Well, let's have a proper look at you then, Annie."

"I told you that suitcase were too heavy for you. We should have asked at station to see if they'd bring it up in the morning." She smiled at him, looking shyly into his brown eyes. This was the man she'd come back home for, and it felt strange . . .

"It would have cost money, them bringing it up to the house. What's in it? Their silver plates?" He laughed.

"Everything," Annie said simply. "But do get your breath back properly — there's no rush to get home."

"Oh, yes, there is." Harold laughed loudly. "I want all the town to see you with me."

Annie had noticed how people who thought they knew her were pretending not to stare as she walked alongside him in her best, well-brushed clothes. Nobody missed a trick round here; everybody always knew everybody else's business and everyone knew that Annie Clegg was back.

"How do, lad! Quite a little lady now, aren't you, Miss Annie Clegg! You'll do well with our Harold, you will." Some of Harold's "butties" from the pit were bawling at them from across the road. They were all laughing and shoving each other, on their way into the Starkie Arms for a pint. Harold nodded, waved and grinned at them.

THE young couple turned off the main street and walked down Peel Terrace. Harry dropped the suitcase again at the front door of the middle house. Then he rattled hard on the brightly polished brass doorknocker. Soon after, the door opened.

"What a din. You'll have all the neighbours out, Harold Calderbank. Oh, Annie, you're home at last. I *have* missed you . . . Come on in, the pair of you, before you freeze. I'll go and put the kettle on. You'll have a cup with us before you go, Harold?" Then Annie's mother noticed the vast suitcase.

"She's not made you carry that big thing up the hill, has she, Harold?"

"She has that and I'm not sorry to put it down, either. Proper bossy, she is," he joked.

"I am not," Annie protested.

Her mother put her arm round her and drew her into the house and Harold followed in behind before putting the case down in the hall.

"Look, I'd best be off, but thanks for the offer of some tea. I'll let you get unpacked and that.

"When are you coming up?" he asked Annie, jerking his head towards his own house.

"I'll come tomorrow afternoon if that's all right with your mam. If it's not, could you call round and tell me before you go on the two o'clock shift?"

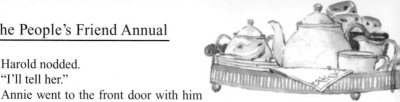

Harold nodded.

"I'll tell her."

Annie went to the front door with him and reached up to give him an awkward little kiss on the cheek while her mam was busy in the kitchen.

Harold looked round quickly to see if there was anybody in the street. There wasn't, so he grabbed her, bent his head down and kissed her properly.

"There, I've been wanting to do that all night," he said proudly.

Annie blushed and rubbed at the side of her face where his rough stubble had stung her cheek.

"That hurt," she said. "You might have had a shave, Harold."

But it didn't stop her giving him another quick kiss before closing the front door behind him, and pushing back the roll of newspapers covered in velveteen that her mam used to keep out the draught at the bottom of the door.

SITTING comfortably at the table with their cups of tea, mother and daughter faced each other.

"So that's it, then — you're back. Oh, I'm that glad, Annie."

"Me, too, Mam. I don't want to polish other people's houses any more, however grand, or to bob and curtsey and all that. I just want to be back where I belong."

"But you are sure about Harold, aren't you, love? You do love him? He's waited long enough for you. You won't let him down now?"

"No, I won't, Mam, I promise. I've done my little bit of wandering now and I know I love him."

"He's a good, solid reliable lad from a respectable family, is Harold. I've always liked him. He'll look after you properly."

"I know that, Mam. I just felt I needed to see something else before I settled down, that's all. He always said he'd wait for me and he has. I've waited for him, too, and saved up a bit of money. I know Harold's the sort who knows his own worth and speaks his own mind. He's sound and I love him. He's right for me, Mam."

Annie thought about Harold as she sipped scalding, strong tea and nibbled at a boiled ham sandwich. He was a warm sort of chap, good-hearted, the type to do anybody a favour. And she'd always liked the way he looked her straight in the eye and told the truth.

＊　　＊　　＊　　＊

Annie set off to see Mrs Calderbank the next afternoon. Her future mother-in-law was one of those women who couldn't abide what she called "showing off." She eyed Annie's new grey gloves meaningfully as Annie carefully slipped them off, and looked hard at the cameo brooch on her coat, but secretly Mrs Calderbank was glad that Harold was marrying such a decent-looking lass.

Annie had a strong will and temper — everybody knew that — but she'd suit Harold very well. She also knew they'd been saving up to get married. Harold had told her. This impressed the strong-minded woman, sitting with her back straight on her kitchen chair in her plain clothes and apron.

When Harold came in through the back door there was a hot high tea ready and waiting for him, keeping warm between two plates on a pan on top of the cooker. He had a good wash and sat down to eat his dinner.

The wedding was discussed at length. It would be a simple affair, family only, at the Methodist Chapel in two weeks' time. This was where Annie and Harold had first danced together, at the Harvest Meat and Potato Pie Supper and Social.

Before Annie left, Mrs Calderbank asked the girl if she would come back again for her tea on the Sunday afternoon and said to ask if her mam would like to come, too.

"My mam's going over to Auntie Joan's, so she'll not be able to come, but she'll be sorry to miss it. I'll come, though, thank you very much. You'll have to come over to see us next."

"I'll look forward to it. You'll have to start calling me Mother soon, lass," the woman replied. This was a real honour. Annie looked startled but pleased at her gesture.

Harold walked her back to her house and she slipped her gloved hand round his arm and marvelled at the warmth that flowed through him into her. At her house, before she went inside, he bent his head and kissed her again.

This kiss was shy at first and then became more passionate. Annie could feel Harold's heart pounding strongly, and her own was racing, too.

Reluctantly, Harold took his leave of her, and she tidied her hair and tried to calm herself down, taking a few deep breaths, before she put the key in the front door.

O N Sunday, the minister, Mr Howcroft, came over to shake her by the hand before the chapel service started. Annie could feel the eyes of the other women looking at her, taking in her clothes, sizing her up and whispering behind their hands. Her mam sat at her side in her plain black coat and hat.

She felt uncomfortable being the centre of so much attention and wished that her mother hadn't chosen to sit so near to the front — but there had been no seats left near the back. A girl came and sat in the opposite pew, and Annie could feel her staring at her. What could that be about?

She sang the rousing hymns, aware of Harold standing in front of her in the choir. He looked very smart, and she liked the way his eyes kept sliding towards her. It warmed her inside. But still she could feel the girl's eyes staring — watching her every move.

Annie turned sideways to see her properly. She was a tough young woman, but not bad looking, and about Annie's own age. Annie didn't *think* she knew her . . .

At the end, there was an excited rustle as people she'd known all her life came over to congratulate her and welcome her back. But the other girl stood upright in her pew, sideways, facing Annie. She was definitely waiting to speak to her.

The two girls remained behind as the rest of the congregation filed out, Annie's mam amongst them, talking to her friend Ethel.

"I'll be going over to Auntie Joan's, love. I'll see you later," she called, knowing Annie would be waiting for Harold to get changed.

Annie sat in the hard pew, ready for the argument that she somehow knew was going to come.

"So you've finally decided you want him, then," the young woman said.

"I have."

"You do know he's been going about with me, don't you?"

"No, I don't, and to tell the truth I'm not in the least bit interested."

"Well, you should be. He's been doing it behind your back, on and off, for a good few months."

Annie wanted to say he must have been hard up but didn't. She felt more surprised than angry. Surely this girl wasn't the type of woman Harold would be interested in?

"Look at you, sitting there and thinking you're better than everybody else in your fancy clothes. Well, I'm here to tell you that Harold Calderbank is not as straightforward as you think he is."

ANNIE refused to say anything more to this girl. She sat and stared straight in front of her, her back and neck stiff and angry. At last Harold came through from the vestry.

"Do you know this young woman, Harold? She says you do," Annie asked, coming straight to the point.

Harold looked guilty, but stood his ground, looking at both women in turn. Then he opened his mouth, but decided to shut it again. He finally said, "This is Ellen Dykes, Annie."

"Well, go on then, Harold Calderbank, tell her. Weren't you going out with me before she decided to come back?" The girl's voice was hoarse with spite.

"It were only on and off, Ellen, and not a bit serious. And it's been over for ages. Ellen knew all about you, Annie, *and* that I was spoken for. She's just out to cause trouble," he said, looking into Annie's face, then at his polished shoes.

"I can see I should have come back sooner," Annie said dryly.

"Happen you should have," he said simply. He looked into her eyes and she knew he was speaking the truth about Ellen Dykes.

"So that's it, I was just your stop gap," Ellen Dykes said. Her face was red as she said to Annie, "You're welcome to him! Me, I wouldn't touch him with a barge pole!" Her voice was still angry as she stalked out of the empty chapel.

"Are you sure it was only for a few weeks, Harold, and that it meant

Peebles, Scotland

*F*RIENDS had long told us of the beauty and wonder of Peebles, but we discovered this hidden treasure for ourselves only a few years ago. My husband was overjoyed with the world-famous salmon fishing in the River Tweed and I was interested to discover that it had an amazing number of exclusive shops.

We were lucky enough to be there during the Beltane Festival in June — a celebration of the return of summer dating from the 15th century — when the whole town seemed to be decked in red and white. The crowning of the Beltane Queen was a highlight, but I especially loved the local schoolchildren who were dressed in traditional costume.

A walk along the river at night was a lovely way to end each day and your wonderful cover made my husband and I feel like we were there all over again!
— **Mrs W.I., Doncaster.**

J. CAMPBELL KERR.

nothing at all to you?" Annie asked quietly, tears in her eyes, but her face stiff and tight. She bent forward to pull on her new grey gloves and sat examining them carefully until she felt calmer.

"I am."

"You've hurt that girl, you know."

"I know and I'm sorry. But it was the truth I spoke. I like her well enough — but I *love* you, Annie."

"Well, then, that's the end of it. Let's be off to your house for our tea."

THEY walked side by side, not touching, not speaking, back to Harold's house. Harold went upstairs to hang his best Sunday jacket carefully on his coat hanger, then he came back downstairs and sat near the fire, his face miserable.

Mrs Calderbank, sensing the tense atmosphere, turned to Annie.

"You come upstairs with me, love, to take your coat off. You've never seen my upstairs, have you? You can leave your coat on the bed, if you want. Tidy your hair and that."

Seeing upstairs in Mrs Calderbank's house was a rare honour, usually only bestowed on relations. She bustled the girl upstairs, glaring at Harold.

"What's the matter now?" his dad said bluntly.

"Annie's found out about Ellen Dykes. She was in church, causing a bit of bother."

"Well it serves you right, lad. You shouldn't have gone off playing wi' fire. It'd serve you right if Annie has nothing more to do with you. You had a proper understanding with her," his dad said unsympathetically.

"It was really nothing with Ellen. It was just for some company. You know I've always loved Annie." Then his dad heard his muffled voice saying, "I know I did wrong," as he stared into the coal fire.

When Annie came back downstairs, she was cheerful and pleasant with all the family. They sat down for a traditional Sunday tea — pie, tinned red salmon, bread and butter, tinned pears, jelly and evaporated milk. There was also a home-made Victoria sponge cake baked by Mrs Calderbank. Annie ate well and Mrs Calderbank noticed and smiled at her approvingly.

Finally, Annie looked up from her plate and looked at Harold. She realised the situation was partly of her own making. If she hadn't gone to work away from home, this would never have happened.

Harold sat facing her, chewing miserably on a slice of pork pie he obviously didn't want to swallow. The tips of his ears were bright red, Annie noticed. She smiled at him, and he managed to smile back.

"Are you enjoying your tea, Harold? That pie looks really good, love," she said with a smile, and it was as though the sun had come out. The whole family relaxed.

"Mrs Dykes is a respectable sort of woman, Annie," Mrs Calderbank ventured. "But her Ellen's always had a yearning for our Harold. You're the one he always wanted though; you know that," she said, patting Annie's hand.

"Do you want me to get your coat, Annie?" Harold asked, obviously relieved at how things were working out.

"No, I don't think so, Harold. I think I'll stop here with Mother and wait for you," she said.

Mrs Calderbank's lined, work-hardened face went pink with pleasure.

"Right, then, I'd better be off then," Harold said. "I'll see you later, will I?"

"You will Harold — *definitely*. I'll walk to the door with you."

IN the vestibule Harold kissed her and she kissed him back just as fervently this time. The feeling of jealousy that had swept over her in the church had made her decided that she was going to keep a tight hold of this man *for ever*.

"I'm sorry," he said.

"It was my fault, too. I shouldn't have gone away in the first place. It's over and done with now. But I'll be keeping my eye on you in future, Harold Calderbank. I don't want to lose you, do I?" She laughed. Then she laid her hand against his smooth, newly-shaved cheek and left it there for a few seconds.

Harold walked off down the street looking pleased. He glanced back and waved, so smart in his best black suit and hat.

She went back to help Mrs Calderbank clear the table and wash the pots in the scullery, leaving Father smoking by the fire. She casually asked the older woman if she'd like to come and look at some second-hand furniture she'd seen for their house on the Wednesday as she dried the pots and stacked them away in the cupboard.

"Yes, love, I'd like that. I wonder — will your mam be coming with us, too? It would be good to know her better. It'll be a nice outing for all three of us women."

"Yes, it will. We'll call for you at two." Annie laughed.

Mrs Calderbank knew then that her Harold had met his match.

Impulsively, she went into the parlour and came back with the spare glass fruit set she'd been keeping in the display cabinet.

"I got two when I were married so you might as well have this one," she said awkwardly.

"Thank you, Mother," Annie said. "It'll come in really useful. I'll take it back home with me when Harold comes back.

"Mam told me right from the start that your Harold was the right lad for me. She was right, too. Mam also said Harold had had a good upbringing and a good mother behind him. I can see she was quite right about that, too."

Mrs Calderbank shook her head dismissively but was really as pleased as Punch.

"I think I'll make us a cup of tea before Harold gets back. Do you want one, love?"

"I do," Annie said, laughing. ■

Daffodils And Dreams

by Em Barnard.

POPPING up from clearing winter debris from beneath her privet hedge, Fliss smiled in greeting as yet another coloured ribbon of coach trippers wandered past on their way to view the daffodils in the woodland beside her cottage. Easter bank holidays always brought them out in droves. She'd been exchanging the usual weather-related comments all day, as well as pointing out the entrance to the less observant.

"Right. A cup of tea, and then a clear up," she said to herself, before stooping to admire a cluster of dainty Jetfire daffs — her favourite. As she set off for the kitchen a voice hailed her. She half turned to see a retired gentleman, burly but well groomed, hurrying towards her hedge. As he opened his mouth again, Fliss beat him to it.

"That way, just follow it round," she said breezily, pointing him towards a trail that nature was determined to conceal. "If you hurry you'll catch the others up."

She swirled round and hurried indoors.

After clicking the kettle on, she glanced through her nets and saw him dithering, looking first down the lane and then at her cottage. She shook her head, annoyed that once again the council had been slacking in pruning back the prolific greenery. There was a bridle path pointer, but unless you had sharp eyesight you could miss that, too. She watched him, his step hastening as he rounded to disappear into the earth-packed pathway.

She gazed a few seconds longer, for he reminded her of someone. Probably Rob, by the way he carried himself, she thought. For her husband had always held himself erect, ready to face, with courage, any hostility dealt him through his vocation.

"Upright to the point of falling backward," she used to say to him.

"Ah," Rob would say. "It puts inches on you. Gives you that air of authority against the scoundrels."

28

Illustration by Stephanie Axtell.

"Oh, yes? Inches round the waist, more like," she'd jest.

"Then you shouldn't feed me so well, my love," he'd reply with a twinkling grin.

The "Dixon Of Dock Green" days were Rob's era.

"I'm glad I'm not in the force today," he'd often declared, when after retirement he'd watch the policemen on the television — real or fictional.

Ah, now could it be that nice Wexford actor that this chap reminded her of? She shook her head, unsure, and made her tea, her thoughts drifting again to Rob. It was September when he'd passed on. He was in her thoughts more so this weekend, for it had been an Easter weekend when she'd first met him in the daffodil wood.

*   *   *   *

She was nineteen. On Good Friday, her boyfriend of two months had told her he'd met someone else. She'd spent Saturday morning moping and being consoled by her best friend, Sheila. In the afternoon Sheila had to go to see

29

her grandparents, so Fliss went into the wood instead.

She left the winding path and crossed the yellow-spangled emerald carpet towards the denser woodland, heading for Oakapple Creek. It was a haunt of the older kids, now ignored by the younger set who congregated around a new amenity centre at the far side of the quaint village, close to the castle. All set up for tourism which, a decade and a half on from the war, was increasing.

There was no-one at the creek and, feeling lonely, she sat and had a little weep.

Next she was staring at a pair of black polished boots, which belonged to a tall, strapping fellow in dark trousers and blazer. He was gripping a bunch of daffodils.

"Are you all right?" he asked.

She nodded, brushing fingers across her wet cheeks.

"For you."

Surprised, her gaze lifted from the daffodils offered and when she met his smiling blue eyes she felt her heart flutter.

"Thank you."

"I'm a policeman — though out of uniform today. I was just checking, making sure no lads had got up to mischief. I remember them fouling up the bank holiday for others last year with their jeering and fighting."

"They don't come here now. They hang about the castle."

"Would you like to walk awhile?" he asked in a soft voice.

She wanted to, but his gaze left her feeling vulnerable, so she said instead, "I'd like to go home." He offered his hand and she took it, feeling the ease in his strength as he pulled her up.

He walked her back to the lane, hardly a word spoken between them, though whenever she peeped over that bunch of daffodils, she found him smiling her way. They arrived at Daffodil Cottage where his cycle leaned into the privet hedge.

"You'll be all right now?"

"Yes — thank you."

He sprung his clips on, bowed gallantly and took his leave.

"I'll be on the first seat along the trail this time tomorrow — if you'd care to take a walk then?"

She gazed after him — her knight in shining armour — as he biked off up the rise and through the Wordsworth public house car park towards the small town three miles away. She turned left and took the path past the cottages that led to her village a mile on. Rob was four years older, but from that first meeting she knew she would marry him.

SHE met him that Sunday afternoon, there amongst the daffodils. She sat on the seat demurely, and in a dress rather than slacks and jumper. Her sleek fair hair nestled into the curve of her shoulders, rather than in a ponytail. Beside her sat Sheila, who'd insisted on coming along, too.

"He's a man, not a boy," Fliss had told her smugly the evening before.

"Then even more reason to have a chaperone, if he's not one of the local lads."

Fliss had looked at Sheila askance. She could have argued that the trail would be alive with chaperones — all those strollers. But feeling a little apprehensive of the meeting, she decided on her friend's support.

"All right. But if you dare to think you're stealing him, Sheila Burton . . ."

"I'll wander off once we've been introduced, stay nearby. Just in case."

"I told you, he's a gentleman."

He was. When introduced to her friend, he nodded politely and would have been happy to allow Sheila to tag along with them. Which she was eager to do until Fliss pinched her arm.

"Haven't you come to pick daffodils for your mum?" she said, smiling sweetly.

Secretly, Fliss was glad her friend was flitting close by, though she was soon at ease with her dark, wavy-haired knight. The trail eventually led them back to Daffodil Cottage.

"Would you care to go to the Calypso Ballroom next Saturday? Your friend, too, if she likes," Rob said.

"She hasn't got a boyfriend," Fliss protested before Sheila could answer. She didn't want her tagging along.

"Then I'll bring you a partner. You'll like Jim."

At first Fliss was a tad jealous, for Jim was like a pea out of the same pod, just as strapping and gallant as Rob. That evening, it was Sheila who wore the smug smiles. Soon, however, they became a foursome.

Over the following months they had fun times at the ballroom, the cinema, picnics in the wood, though now and then Fliss would catch Jim staring at her. He'd smile, and Fliss would give a shy smile back and cosy up to Rob.

Sometimes, when in the woodland, the girls couldn't believe that the two men could be such boys, for they climbed trees and fought, Rob pushing Jim into nettles, Jim pelting his pal with crab apples.

"It's just like they've been let out of junior school rather than the police force," Sheila remarked with a roll of her eyes, as they sat dangling legs on a low horizontal limb of a distorted oak.

ONE day in the summer Jim shocked them by revealing that he was transferring to London.

"But why — you never said?" Sheila was more surprised than upset.

"Just time to move on. There's no chance of promotion in a small town like this."

"True," Rob said, then went quiet after catching Fliss's look of alarm. "I wish you luck, Jim."

"Sheila'll be all right," Fliss said, as her friend wandered off and Jim followed. "It's not like she's in love with him."

When the day neared to leave, Jim sat pensive, staring out over the pond.

"What's up, Jim?" Rob asked airily, as he skimmed stones across its murky waters. "Wishing you weren't going?"

"I shall miss coming here with all of you, yes. Think I'll write a letter, put all my dreams and memories of these times in a bottle and stick it in that old oak at the far side of the pond."

"You'll never make it," Rob scoffed. "It may look glassy clear on top but it's deep mud beneath." Rob pelted a crab apple at his pal — blithely unaware that his direct hit had knocked Jim's gaze that had transferred to Fliss.

"Then when we're old and grey we can get our grandchildren to retrieve them, eh, Fliss?" Sheila said.

Fliss drew her eyes from Jim and beamed her friend a smile.

"Then we'll do the same, won't we, Fliss?" Rob said. "Oakapple Creek will always belong to the four of us then."

"I know what I'm going to put in mine," Sheila said, and bent into Fliss to confide her secret yearnings.

April Blossom

*A*N April shower!
   Little hailstones bounce,
Grey-fluff clouds have gathered,
Windblown petals flounce!
Cats all run for shelter,
The sunshine hides away,
Skies bring ice and water,
It's a splendid April day!

✳   ✳   ✳   ✳

The following day saw Rob beating his friend to teeter across submerged stones and slimy logs to reach the far edge. He then began his climb to gasps of horror from the girls as rotting branches crackled and snapped under his grasp. But the cheers went up as he sat atop the mast.

"There's a ledge to sit them on," he called, having peered into the dark hollow. He retrieved, from his pocket, the two bottles that belonged to Fliss and himself and placed them inside. He then returned to the others.

Jim went next — after a good luck kiss from Sheila — and all went well until he began his descent. A sudden snap underfoot had the branch plummeting earthwards, followed by Jim, arms flailing and landing belly down in an explosion of water.

"Jim!" Sheila squealed, hands across mouth.

Jim hauled himself up, rivulets of water draining from him.

"Don't just stand there!" he yelled before toppling backwards for another drenching.

Rob, who was roaring and slapping his hands on his knees, jumped into action. Precariously stepping across the stones, he balanced on a log, stretched out a hand and hauled Jim out. The girls stared, horrified, as

32

T.G. Hopewell.

*Showers to make spring
    flowers grow,
And give the birds a drink,
As all the lovely blossoms
    dance
Silk-white and pretty pink.
Daffodils are nodding wisely,
For, though the cloudtops
    tower,
Sunshine follows on behind;
It's just an April shower!*

— *Enid Pearson.*

wobbling and holding fast to each other the two pals made it back to the bank.

Then one of the group, though no-one could quite remember who, burst into a giggle. Jim, dripping, his face speckled in peaty matter, was the only one who didn't see the funny side of it as they headed for home that last day. When they came out of the wood, Jim was still extracting pond life from his clothes and hair.

"You OK?" Rob asked, concerned. As Jim nodded, he added humorously, "Well, you're not likely to forget our last day together now, eh, Jim?"

Jim looked at each of his friends in turn.

"I would never have forgotten anyway," he said, his eyes landing on Fliss.

✳   ✳   ✳   ✳

After that, with the foursome broken up and Sheila not wanting to play gooseberry, Fliss and Rob were left to their courting.

"I hope to make superintendent one day," Rob confided as they walked from the autumn woodland into the sunlight one afternoon.

Fliss gazed over the gate of the cottage as Rob clipped tight his trouser legs.

"All I want is to be a mother of four children, two of each, and keep house here at Daffodil Cottage."

It almost worked to order. Three children became their quota. Rob didn't quite fulfil his dream. But Daffodil Cottage came up for sale, allowing Fliss to fulfil hers. They'd had such a wonderful life together, and the cottage was perfect.

FLISS took her tea on to the patio, and the radio, too. Listening to some Chopin from the seclusion of her trellis where twining roses and clematis would soon bloom again, she watched the visitors gradually wander homeward. After a while those particular coach trippers to whom the gentleman belonged also filed past. Her search for him proved he was lagging again.

She yawned, stood and stretched her back, then went indoors, refilled her kettle, and clicked it on. Watching for him from her window while drinking tea and nibbling at a scone, she passed an impatient ten minutes.

As she spotted the last coach drive off, her concern grew. The sun was dipping, bathing the countryside in a rich golden hue — the day was drawing in. Those passing her cottage became few and far between, which had her wondering if he'd become ill, or had tripped somewhere.

She decided to take a stroll herself — she often did so in the cool and quiet of the evening. Her mind was throwing up all kinds of misfortunes that might have become him. She shuffled on a coat and set off.

A chill invaded her bones as she entered the shade of that concealed entrance. After twenty metres the trail broke free from dense woodland to wind through an open combination of daffodil-studded meadow and airy woodland.

She came upon the profusion of primroses and periwinkles that signified the pathway to Oakapple Creek. It was long gone now, that trail, since the council's woodland committee had insisted visitors kept to the pathways. But she took it anyway, some sixth sense urging her across the meadow towards Oakapple Creek.

The dark reaches of the denser woodland held no fear for her. It was home ground and always would be. Coming towards the creek, the evening sun burnishing the glassy pond copper, she was halted in her step. Peering through the trees she saw a dark, ominous form, hunched, arms held out from its sides like a drowned bird, and muttering to itself. Her own wary form soon relaxed as a memory flashed before her.

"Jim!" She hastened towards him, peering into the cheery mud-splattered face that suddenly appeared from behind the white handkerchief, now stained brown.

"It *is* you! Are you all right?" She looked him up and down. "Goodness! You haven't . . .? You didn't . . .?" She stared past him to the pond.

"Not quite, Fliss." He chuckled. "I'd been sitting a while, reflecting, but then I went in a bit too close to the pond and tripped. Seems it's still out to get me, that morass."

Fliss stared at his mud-plastered front. She gave a chuckle.

"It's like we've gone back forty-odd years. Why didn't you say something when we spoke earlier on?"

"You hardly gave me a chance, Fliss! So I thought I'd wander the old haunts first, then call in on the way back." He thwacked his arms, and dollops of mud pattered like a shower on to the damp leafy carpet. He shook his head at the sorry state of himself.

"Come on, Jim, back to the cottage," she said stretching out an embracing arm, then thinking better of it. She walked alongside him. "You can have a shower and I'll sort you out with some of Rob's clothes. At least they'll fit."

✳   ✳   ✳   ✳

"I adore my garden, but this weekend has been its usual nightmare," she explained, setting a tray on the coffee table.

Jim relaxed in a comfy chair, the whirr of the washing machine in the background. He was now scrubbed clean and warmly clad, his steel-grey thatch of hair sleeked back and shining wet from his shower.

"It's always the same on bank holidays — the council never remembers to prune that entrance. I'm constantly being asked by visitors just where to go."

"Which is almost what you told me to do." Jim chuckled as he accepted the proffered tea.

"Oh, I'm sorry, Jim. I thought you were part of that coach party. I just didn't recognise you."

"But you did once I had mud all over me!"

Fliss smiled as she patted a cushion and sat down.

"So do you think they're still there?"

"Who? Oh, our four bottles. Goodness knows. I remember Rob — just after we married — wanting to retrieve them. Ours, that is — we wouldn't have disturbed yours and Sheila's. But we decided against it. It would have been like breaking up the foursome."

She offered him the plate of fruit scones.

"We did confide in each other, though, on what we put in our letters." She smiled, remembering. "There was nothing surprising — just the usual lovey-dovey stuff and what we hoped for in the future. Which basically came true."

"I remember exactly what I wrote — and it holds to this day," Jim said, quietly reflective as he manoeuvred his scone to dead centre of his plate.

"It was a sort of . . . confession, I suppose you might call it."

As a silence followed he looked up.

"One day, Fliss, I might explain. One day."

FLISS found her gaze locked into Jim's. He was giving her that same intense look he used to give her when the four of them were together. She'd pretended back then that it hadn't meant anything, but if the truth were told, she'd known that if Rob hadn't stolen her heart Jim could easily have done so. She drew her cup and saucer to her chest and sipped her tea.

"So," she said, feeling the need to change the subject, "is it just a sentimental journey that's brought you this way again?"

"As a matter of fact I've moved back to the area. I've a bungalow down Ash Grove Lane, close to where I used to live. The family's spread around the country, so I decided to come home. At least I'm closer to David than I was in Surrey. He's my youngest."

Fliss nodded, understanding.

"Our Rick is in the States, but the other two are local."

"Well, Fliss, as I'm now . . . local, I wondered if maybe you and I . . ."

"Ah, that's the machine finished." Fliss jumped up, glad of the moment to collect her thoughts.

Half an hour later they stood in the hall saying their farewells.

"So . . . Could I see you again, Fliss?"

She passed him his clothes in a carrier. She could feel a fluttering in her heart — she knew where they would be heading if she agreed. She looked into his eyes, and smiled.

"Yes, Jim," she said easily.

THAT autumn, for their umpteenth meeting since their reunion, Fliss and Jim took a stroll into the woodland, their steps automatically leading them to Oakapple Creek.

"I don't quite know how to go about this, Fliss — though probably you know what I'm about to ask you." Jim said, standing and staring at the tree. "But before that," he added quickly, "I want to tell you the contents of that letter."

"Jim, you don't have to."

He found her hand and gripped it.

"But I do. I remember every word. It's never left me." He took a breath and began.

"I need to write it down, the sadness I feel today. Not only for leaving the woodland and my dearest friends, but also because I love one of you more than the others. It's you, my darling Fliss — you've captured my heart. But the love I see in your eyes is for Rob. And it's because I don't ever want to hurt either of you that I have to go away. For good."

Fliss sighed.

"Oh, Jim. I knew you felt something for me, but I never suspected that that was why you left!" She turned to him. "Was that why your letters petered out, too?"

Jim nodded, smiling wistfully. She gripped his hand in both of hers and dipped her head, feeling suddenly embarrassed over her coming words.

"If it hadn't been for Rob, you know . . ."

Jim set his other hand on top of hers.

"Oh, Rob was always the one for you, Fliss. I couldn't have won you back then — and anyway, Rob was my best pal. And if I'd stayed . . . well, one day I might have slipped, shown the love I felt for you, and hurt us all. I couldn't take that chance, Fliss."

They stood in silence some moments, the wind flurrying autumn leaves around them, and stared at the oak beyond the pond where the bottles sat within.

"Fliss." Jim waited till her eyes met his. "My love for you still holds firm. I did find another love and I have a beautiful family through it. But my wife passed on some years back.

"And then I read about Rob. That's why I returned, in the hope that . . . What I'm asking, Fliss, my darling, is . . . would you do me the honour now of becoming my wife?"

Fliss had known his sincerity for too long to hesitate.

"Yes, Jim, I will," she replied. ■

Ebbw Vale Festival Park, Wales

*W*HEN I saw Ebbw Vale Festival Park on your cover I was
delighted to see what regeneration has done for this once grimy
mining and industrial town. The last time I was there was in my
boyhood for a family visit.

I never used to believe my grandfather when he told me of seeing
real Native American Indian families camped in the town. But then I
learned that "Buffalo Bill" Cody brought his Wild West Show to
Britain to mark Queen Victoria's Golden Jubilee, and appeared at the
Palace Theatre And Cinema!

— *Mr K.G., Queensland, Australia.*

J. CAMPBELL KERR.

IT was the pile of books in the window that had lured me into the charity shop that Monday, just over a year ago now. I work in the local library, you see, and Monday is my day off, to compensate for working Saturdays.

Not that doing Saturdays bothers me. I love my job. I'll read anything and all those shelves of books — it's like being in heaven!

At Christmas, given my love of reading, everyone gives me book tokens and I'd just recently replenished my own personal mini-library at home. But even by then — the beginning of February, and icy cold — I'd already got through them and was on the lookout for more. And since I was also still recovering from my own seasonal expenditure, the charity shop's offerings held particular appeal!

So I went in to buy a couple of books to keep me going and it became a bit of a habit. I got to know the staff — all volunteers — and by July, when they were a bit short of people because of holidays, I ended up volunteering myself.

At first, I just had it in mind to help out over the summer, but, there we were, February again, and I was still turning up to do my weekly Monday morning shift . . .

A Good Place To Start

by Val Bonsall.

"HOW are you today?" Donald asked, as I hurried in from the biting wind.

"Fine," I replied. I smiled at him and Kate, who both looked about to collapse under the huge pile of stuff they were each carrying. "And you two look in the pink!"

Donald was a teacher, mostly at evening classes,

which is why he was often free to volunteer during the day, and Kate was retired. It was Kate who twigged first that I'd been making a joke. In the pink, you see, because virtually everything in their arms was pink.

"It's for our Valentine window display," she said.

"Valentine?"

"It's Valentine's Day on Wednesday."

"Is it?" I did a quick calculation. "Yes, you're right. I'd forgotten. Or just not thought about it, I guess."

"I hadn't thought about it, either," Kate agreed, "but Donald reminded me."

She gave me a look. Amused, but not unkindly so. She reckoned Donald fancied me.

Maybe he did, but I just thought of him as a workmate. Well, a friend, too, I guess, but that was all.

I had an eye open for Mr Right and I was certain I'd know it was him the moment I first saw him.

Like my grandad Bayley. He said the first time he saw my grandma — at a bus-stop, on a frosty, moonlit night — he knew immediately she was The One. He got on the bus after her, even though he'd no idea where it was going! Cupid's arrow, straight in the heart, he said.

But Donald — I couldn't even remember when he started helping at the shop. Had he been one of the team that were there that first day I'd gone in? I hadn't a clue. However, I did agree that it was a good idea of his to do up the window.

Kate and I dressed a female dummy, head to toe, in donated pink clothing. Then we did a male, in a dark suit and silky pink tie.

Meanwhile, Donald and a young French woman called Claudette, who'd

recently volunteered, cut big heart-shapes out of cardboard. They dangled them on ribbons from the top of the window, where they danced in the breeze from the solitary fan-heater that was struggling to keep us warm.

Donald then went out and came back with a bottle of wine.

Claudette carefully examined the label then smiled enthusiastically.

"Yes, zis is nice wine, Don-ald."

I smiled, too. We all loved her accent.

Illustration by Rossan.

By then we'd been joined by another volunteer, Hal, who was nearly ninety and lived just round the corner. He greeted us by questioning whether we could sell the wine when we changed the window in a few days' time.

"That depends on whether Don . . ." Kate began.

"No, no!" Hal gave a dismissive wave of his hand. "I mean, could you sell it legally? Would you need a temporary licence, it being alcohol?"

Trust Hal. He thinks of everything!

Donald grinned.

"Can't you just see the local paper's headline? *Charity shop workers jailed for flouting licensing laws!*" He waved his hands as he spoke, as though writing the headline.

That got us all laughing, which is one of the things I like about working here — we always have a laugh together.

Donald decided to put the bottle of wine on a little side-table that someone had given, and we found a couple of glasses from a box of donated kitchen stuff. He then went out to the newsagent next door and came back with a *Be My Valentine* card. He put it in the middle of the table before we positioned the dummies, in their finery, on either side.

"A romantic dinner for two," Kate said.

Donald nodded in reply to her, but I felt his eyes on me.

LATER, when Kate and Claudette were busy with customers, he came up to where I was sorting out the rest of the kitchen-stuff box.

"I got the idea," he said, pointing vaguely in the direction of the window, "because I won a prize draw at work and I now have a voucher for two special Valentine's Day meals at that little restaurant under the bridge." He took an invitation from his pocket. There was a picture on it that looked very much like our display.

"Have you ever been there," he continued, "to the restaurant?"

"I 'ave. When I first arrive 'ere," Claudette interrupted. She'd finished serving her customer and had come over to where we were. *"Très bon!"* She nodded her approval.

I was just grateful for her intervention. I was sure, if she hadn't appeared, Donald would have asked me to go with him for this "special Valentine meal" and, like I said, I just didn't see him in that way.

More customers then came in — several of whom were full of praise for our display — and we were all busy until I left at one o'clock.

I managed to sneak out without Donald noticing as Claudette was busy talking to him about the restaurant again.

As I crossed the road, I saw Martyn Blanes coming out of the office that bore his name above the door.

Now with Martyn, on the other hand, I could remember exactly when I first saw him, no problem. I'd been about to cross the road one wet Monday when he'd brushed past me. I'd just stood there, transfixed, thinking how handsome he was!

If he'd invited me out . . .

✳　　✳　　✳　　✳

I'd taken the rest of the week off work, to use up my odd days, and on the Tuesday I spring-cleaned my little house. A bit early, I know, but I hadn't lived there long and it was my pride and joy!

Then, on the Wednesday, while I was still in the mood, I went round to my parents' to make sure theirs was all clean, tidy and welcoming, too. They were due back at the weekend from a five-week trip to Australia, where they'd been visiting an old friend of Mum's.

I'd just got home and sat down with a cup of tea — vaguely thinking about Martyn Blanes — when there was a knock on the door.

I opened it, and there was a huge bunch of roses being held aloft by a tiny little man.

"Valentine present, I think." He beamed at me. "Will you just sign this?" He pushed a clipboard in front of me, and pointed to my address, about halfway down the page.

I borrowed his pen and scribbled my name. He then got back in his van and drove off.

Donald, of course! The meal he'd talked about on Monday was just the most recent in a series of hints.

I didn't want to, because I was worried about how it would affect things at the shop, but I knew I wasn't going to be able to avoid telling him how I felt — or more importantly, how I didn't feel — for much longer.

Possibly not for any longer, if he was starting to send me big bunches of flowers!

I WAS so sure that the flowers had come from Donald that I'd taken them into the living-room and was starting to remove the outer wrapping before I looked at the little gift-tag.

And they weren't from Donald . . .

They weren't even for me! The little tag read, *To Ellie, From Adam xxx*.

Ellie — my younger sister by ten years — was staying with me while our parents were in Australia.

But who, I wondered, was Adam?

I didn't have to wait long to find out.

"Adam? Oh, he's just a guy at school." Ellie, who had returned from school a couple of minutes later, sniffed at the bouquet. Then she looked about her. "Has any post come here for me? Cards?"

"No."

"Oh." Definite dismay in her voice. "I popped in at home and there was

nothing there for me, either."
She frowned.

"Don't be so greedy!" I laughed. "Adam's sent you a beautiful bunch of flowers. What more do you want?"

She looked at me solemnly.

"I'd hoped Danny might send me something."

"Danny?" Suddenly it dawned. "Danny, round the corner from here?"

She nodded her head. I shook mine. I knew the Danny she meant and I did not much care for him. Maybe it was just a rebellious phase he was going through, the way he was always pushing his luck, but for the moment, he was not what you'd choose for your kid sister.

Suddenly it occurred to me that I might have met Adam, too.

"That concert you were in at Christmas —" Ellie is into music and a member of the school orchestra "— this Adam came to see it, didn't he? He sat next to me and Grandma Bayley?"

"Probably." Ellie threw back her head in a weary gesture. "He's always around, like a shadow, or a faithful old sheepdog, you know?"

"He seemed nice to me."

"He is. As a friend. But not, you know, romantically, if you understand."

Step Back In Time

Robert Burns

ROBERT BURNS, or Rabbie, as he is more affectionately known, is the national poet of Scotland.

Born in Alloway, South Ayrshire on January 25, 1759, to self-educated tenant farmers William Burnes and Agnes Broun, Burns was the eldest of seven children.

Although he is better known by his shortened surname, Burns used his father's surname until 1786 — two years after William died.

Burns had little regular schooling and obtained much of his education from his father who taught Robert and his siblings reading, writing, arithmetic, geography and history, although Robert went on to have a more formal education while his father took on tenancy at Mount Oliphant farm, south-east of Alloway.

Burns's early life was full of poverty and hardship. This left its mark in later life as Burns was blighted with a premature stoop and weakened constitution — factors which contributed to his premature death at just thirty-seven.

After his schooling, Burns became a labourer and, by fifteen, he was the head labourer at Mount Oliphant.

It was here that he was inspired to write "Handsome Nell" for Nellie Kilpatrick — his first attempt at poetry.

She nodded again, wisely, as though she — all seventeen years of her — was a world expert on all things romantic!

But I did understand. I was in exactly the same situation.

Or was I?

When Ellie went off to put the flowers in a vase, I started wondering about that.

The family moved to Tarbolton where, to his father's disapproval, Burns joined a country dancing school and co-founded the Tarbolton Bachelors' Club.

Burns went on to write hundreds of poems and songs — often influenced by the many women he wooed throughout his life.

He died on July 21, 1796, after intemperance aggravated his long-standing heart condition. However, his legacy lives on.

All over the world, on January 25 — Robert's birthday — people celebrate his life and work with Burns suppers where there are poetry recitals, a traditional Scottish meal and, of course, a toast to the immortal memory of the man himself. ■

I'd not had much time to think about it before, because Ellie had arrived moments after I'd seen the gift-tag, but I'd been convinced the flowers were for me.

From my "old faithful" who was "always around".

But they weren't. And I realised, with another shock, that I was a bit disappointed that they weren't.

I remember Claudette coming over to us when Donald was telling me about the little restaurant. She'd kept saying how much she liked it there.

And, all at once, I was very aware of Claudette's distinctly French . . . what is it they say . . . chic? Donald couldn't fail to be charmed by her; we all were in some way.

She'd been talking to him again when I'd left. What if he'd invited her to share the meal? Would that have bothered me, too?

Maybe it was a case of not appreciating something until you felt you might lose it, but I began to realise that it would bother me.

Ellie came back in then, holding not one, but two vases to take all the roses.

"I bet they cost a fortune," she said. She sighed. "I just don't know what to do."

"You must at least phone Adam and thank him," I said. "And so he knows you've got them."

"Phone? But what if he asks me out or something?"

"That's up to you. But all this stuff about just liking him as a friend — friendship can be a pretty good place to start. It can often become something more, you know . . ."

My voice trailed off. I wasn't just speaking to Ellie — I was telling myself something as well. Maybe my "you'll know the minute you see him" theory wasn't quite what I'd thought it was. I could remember the first time I saw Martyn Blanes, and I was impressed by his good looks, but at the time, he'd been arguing with a parking attendant about his car being in a bay that was clearly marked as allocated for disabled drivers. Martyn was, I suspected, another Danny. Another one for pushing it.

"Phone him?" Ellie repeated again, as though I'd suggested she fly to the moon or something. "Really?"

IT seemed that the phone had been ringing for ever. But at last he answered it.

"Oh, hi, Donald," I said. "Erm . . . that prize you won. You know, the Valentine's Day meal tonight?" I paused, not sure how to continue.

But, as it turned out, I didn't have to.

"Would you like to come?" he asked. "I wanted to ask you at the shop, but it was too busy. Seven-thirty OK?"

We arranged to meet outside.

We had a terrific time. The change of location seemed to make all the difference. When Kate and one or two others at the shop had noticed that he seemed to like me, they'd teased me about it, and I immediately became defensive.

I'm the kind of person who gets embarrassed easily, and I can't remember my exact words, but I would definitely have told them not to be daft and, likely, if they'd persisted, how I didn't fancy him anyway. Maybe, having said that, I'd felt I had to stick to it?

I don't know.

But he had been there waiting for me, and I remember clearly how he looked.

There wasn't any moonlight — like in Grandad's first glimpse of Grandma — but there was a lovely warm glow coming from a lamp beside the restaurant door, and it seemed to shine off him and spread right across to me.

The food was nice and the puddings all had mad names like Sweetheart Strawberry Surprise and Cupid's Custard Kisses. I have to say, I don't know about the custard, but I enjoyed the kisses at the end of the night!

✳   ✳   ✳   ✳

If you're wondering whether we ever did sell the bottle of wine when we changed the display at the shop, and thereby risk flouting the licensing laws, the answer is no.

It hung around in the back for a good few months, then we all had a glass — Kate, Hal, Claudette, Donald and I — when Donald and I got engaged.

If you're wondering about Ellie and Adam, that didn't get off the ground. But, then, neither did Ellie and Danny, so that was OK, too! ■

A Second Chance

by Joanna Barnden.

HANNAH climbed the gracious steps up to the beautiful old hall feeling the mixture of excitement and emotion that a wedding always seemed to provoke in her these days. She expected this one to be even more emotional than most, for today Rachael, her best friend from school, was the bride.

They'd become friends at the age of five, united as the only two Jewish girls in their class, but they'd soon discovered other mutual loves; reading, swimming, shopping — and, of course, boys!

They'd been with each other all the way through kiss-chase at primary school, to shy Valentine cards, to first dates . . . They'd giggled late into the night over who fancied whom and, as they grew older, they'd been there to cushion each other's broken hearts. That had mainly been Rachael, mind you, for Hannah had met Tom at sixteen and still been with him when, at eighteen, all three of them had gone off to college.

Hannah hadn't seen as much of Rachael after that — and nothing of Tom.

She clasped her pashmina around her shoulders, suddenly feeling the chill and wishing she had someone to go in with. *Hannah and friend* the invitation had said, but she'd split up with her most recent "friend" just last month, so she was here alone.

"It'll be fine," Rachael had assured her. "There's a few of the old crowd going so you won't be on your own."

Hannah hadn't dared ask if Tom would be amongst the few and Rachael hadn't said — she'd been too full of the flowers and the dress.

"Good evening, madam."

Hannah nodded to the scarlet-coated Master of Ceremonies as he welcomed her into the beautiful hall. It was already full of people, women elegant in evening dresses, men smart in black tie, cream *kipa* perched respectfully on the back of their heads. Hannah glanced around as everyone moved slowly towards the garden room where the *chuppah* — the wedding canopy — was set up for the ceremony and, to her great relief, saw one of the promised "old crowd".

"Maddy!"

Her friend turned and her face lit up in recognition.

"Hannah! It's so good to see you! This is James, my husband."

Maddy indicated a sandy-haired man beside her who grinned shyly.

A husband, Hannah thought. You, too?

Before she could say anything, however, Maddy was talking again.

"Isn't this wonderful, Han? We've never been to a Jewish wedding before."

Hannah smiled.

"You're in for quite a treat, then."

She'd gone through a phase of hating being Jewish when she was a teenager and her parents' religion had stopped her going out on a Friday night. It had come to a head at the age of eighteen, with her dad's incessant talk of marriage, and for years after she'd left home, Hannah had shunned the Jewish way of life as much as she could. These days, though, some eight years later, she was finding herself returning to the fold. She'd found a local synagogue and been to a few social events. She supposed she must be getting old because suddenly she was finding the familiar routines soothing and the warmth of the people very pleasant after a harsh day's work.

She hadn't gone as far as dating a Jewish man, though — not since Tom.

46

Just then they stepped into the garden room and Maddy gasped.

"Oh! It's beautiful."

It was. The *chuppah* stood in the large bay window, draped in soft muslin and strings of creamy flowers. Chairs were ranged around, a central section facing the canopy and two others to the sides, facing into the room. Maddy looked round, confused, as a group of men filed past them, heading for the far side.

"Do we sit separately?" she asked uncertainly.

Hannah nodded.

"Yep. Girls here, men over there."

"Oh!" Maddy looked at James. "That's a shame."

"Isn't it?" The voice came from behind them and both girls spun round.

"Tom!" Maddy squealed. "Gosh, Rachael really has invited the old crowd."

"Hello, Maddy." He clasped her hands. "It's lovely to see you again after all this time. And Hannah . . ."

He stared at her and Hannah felt herself flush. He looked good. Taller than she recalled but his eyes were the same soft brown she remembered from her first dreams.

The shock of seeing him was so electric it almost stopped her heart.

"Tom, I . . ."

She could find nothing to say, but luckily just then the Master of Ceremonies came up behind them.

"Could we take our places, ladies and gents, please? The bride and groom will be with us shortly."

Tom was whisked away, absorbed by the male crowd and carried off to the far side of the room, leaving Hannah to the safety of the women as she struggled to compose herself.

"It was just a shock seeing him again," she told herself. "Nothing more than that." But if that were the case, why was her heart beating so hard beneath her silk dress?

"Tom looks good these days," Maddy commented beside her. "Mind you, he always did."

"I used to think so," Hannah managed.

"Used to?"

Hannah squirmed as her old friend raised an eyebrow at her.

"Used to," she confirmed, but she couldn't help sneaking another look over at him, just to be sure.

✳   ✳   ✳   ✳

Hannah had met Tom at what she'd been convinced would be a hideous social her mother had organised in the summer of his sixteenth birthday. He'd just moved to their street and would be in her class once school started back and, with him being Jewish as well, her mum had insisted she be nice to him.

Hannah had been determined to be no such thing, but once they'd actually met it had been impossible not to.

He'd kissed her three weeks later in the gathering dusk, on a romantic spot by the river, and by the time school went back, they were a firm couple, rarely out of each other's company.

"It'll end in tears," Rachael had warned, "same class, same street, same synagogue! Imagine how hideous it'll be when you split up!"

"We won't split up," Hannah had replied — and they hadn't. Well, not until they were no longer in the same town, let alone the same street.

Spring Is Here!

*T*HIS *morning, much to my delight,*
I saw a very welcome sight,
Spring had come to clear the air
And spread her wonders everywhere.
She looked around and shook her heac
"There's such a lot to do," she said.
"This wintry scene is far from bright,
It needs a touch of warming light."

"HERE she comes!"

Maddy nudged Hannah, interrupting her reverie, and together they peered down the long corridor to where they could just see a glimpse of cream silk starting towards them. Then, suddenly, there was Rachael.

"She looks lovely," Maddy breathed.

"And so grown up!"

Rachael looked perfect in a long, slim gown, her dark hair in curls, her face mysterious behind the large veil her husband-to-be would have just put in place in the private "bedecken" ceremony upstairs. He had entered ahead of her and was now waiting beneath the canopy as Rachael moved slowly towards him on her father's arm. When she reached him she began to circle him slowly seven times.

When they were younger, Rachael and Hannah had always giggled over this bit of the ceremony, convinced they'd feel really silly, but watching now it seemed to Hannah rather beautiful after all. She watched as Ben, the groom, turned his head, waiting for his bride to come round, and saw how their eyes locked in secret intimacy before she moved away again. Maybe, if it was the right man, this didn't seem silly at all. She wouldn't know. She hadn't found hers yet, and even when she did he probably wouldn't be Jewish.

Involuntarily, her eyes slid towards Tom and she was startled to find his on

And so she swept the clouds away,
Creating such a sunny day
That all the flowers began to grow,
A gentle breeze began to blow,
Which blew away the winter scene
And turned the trees a verdant green.
And, happy with the work she'd done,
She said, "Now winter's really gone!"

— *Alice Drury.*

her. For a second it was as if the last eight years apart had never been, but then the rabbi began chanting the blessing and she was pulled back to the present.

Once finished, the rabbi reached for a cup.

"Now the couple will share a glass of wine," he announced. "Wine is the symbol of joy and joy is the cornerstone of marriage."

"Wow," Maddy breathed beside Hannah, "that's so . . . so modern."

"Is it?"

"Yes! Not 'duty' or 'responsibility' or even 'love', but 'joy'! That's spot on, that is! Everyone should get to have joy, shouldn't they?"

Hannah felt a shiver run down her spine. She hadn't felt a lot of joy recently, if she was honest. Fun, maybe, in a determined, noisy party sort of a way. Satisfaction, yes, with her recent promotion and the new flat it had allowed her to buy. But joy? Things had felt rather empty since she'd split up with Rod. Since before that, in fact, she acknowledged. He'd never been right for her really — not many of them had. Never, in fact, had she felt joy — bubbly, giggly, all's-well-in-the-world joy. Never, at least, since Tom.

"That's rubbish," she told herself sternly as the rabbi began chanting again. "You're just feeling all sentimental because it's a wedding and because he's here and it's shocked you."

Nevertheless, she couldn't stop her mind drifting back to those two idyllic teenage years of picnics and boat trips and fancy dress parties, and hour after hour of sitting on the climbing frame in her back garden just talking, kissing, laughing. So much laughing. Until the end.

Rachael and Ben were exchanging rings now. Her veil went back and Hannah could see her dear old friend's face. Rachael looked radiant and, as she gazed into her new husband's eyes, her own shimmered with love — total, certain, absolute love.

Hannah sucked in her breath with sudden jealousy. Rachael had always been the flighty one. It was she, Hannah, who'd always been constant, certain, loved — so where had it gone wrong?

"And now," the rabbi said, "Rachael's father, David, will sing the *Bessman Tov*."

Looking shy but determined, David took the microphone and began to chant, his voice a little uncertain at first but growing in strength as he sang out the blessing to his daughter and new son. Hannah felt tears prick at her eyes. How her dad would love to be able to do that for her, to see her settled and happy and safe. Looking back now, she could see that that was all he'd wanted when she was a teenager, too. She hadn't seen it like that at the time, though.

✳   ✳   ✳   ✳

"How dare you!" she'd exploded, blazing with eighteen-year-old fury.

It was late. Hannah had just seen Tom out and he'd been nervous and awkward. She'd thought she'd upset him until he'd confessed about the conversation he'd just had with her father.

"I dare," her father had said, drawing himself up, all self-righteous and Jewish, "because I love you and I want the best for you."

"I can manage that myself, Dad! This is *my* relationship. Tom is *my* boyfriend and if he wants to ask me to marry him I'd rather he did it himself than under instruction from you."

"But he does want to, angel. He told me, he . . ."

"Of course he told you, he's terrified of offending you!"

"Did he ask you?"

"Yes."

"He's a good boy."

"This is such good news!" Her mum had leapt up then, ready to embrace her. "We'll have such a ceremony. Oh, darling, I'm so . . ."

"I said no."

"What?"

"He didn't mean it. He was just being dutiful. We're too young. We're going to college — different colleges. We can't get married."

"But, Hannah, don't you love him?"

"I . . ."

She'd faltered then but not for long. She was eighteen years old and she was sick of her parents trying to control her life. She was ready to stand alone.

"We're too young," she'd repeated and then she'd fled, unable to bear the disappointment in their faces.

RACHAEL'S father had finished. Everyone clapped uproariously as he blushed and slid back in beside his wife.

"And now, the groom will break the glass," the rabbi told them, "symbolising how fragile marriage is and how hard a couple must work to keep it safe in their hands."

"Now that's even more modern," Maddy said. "Isn't that what counsellors all over the world tell us now? Your lot knew it thousands of years ago."

Hannah laughed as Ben brought his heel down on the glass and the room echoed with sudden cries of, *"Mazel Tov!"*

"I suppose we did," she agreed. "It doesn't stop us forgetting sometimes, though," she added.

Maddy looked at her strangely.

"You with anyone, Han?"

"Not right now."

"Shame. Tom seems to be here alone, too."

"Does he?" Hannah aimed for sarcasm but didn't make it. She felt her heartbeat quicken again. "Let's not get carried away, Mads," she said quickly, to cover her confusion.

ON'T do this, Hannah," he'd pleaded.

They were on the climbing frame again, in the moonlight, no doubt with her parents peeping out from their bedroom window at them. It was two weeks after the proposal fiasco and the last night before they went off to separate colleges, separate towns — separate lives. Tom didn't want the last one.

"We can do this," he went on. "We can stay together. We're meant to be. I know we are."

"How do we know that, Tom?" Hannah had replied as coldly as she could manage. Seeing him upset like this was killing her, but she had to stick to her guns. "How can we possibly know that until we've seen what else is out there?"

He'd sucked in his breath then, shocked at her callous approach, but she was right, she knew she was. She did love Tom, but they were so young! Neither of them had ever been out with anyone else.

"What if we are right for each other," he persisted, "but we separate now and never see each other again? We'll have missed out on so much."

"No, Tom, that's not right," she'd insisted. "If we are right for each other we *will* meet again."

✳   ✳   ✳   ✳

And now here they were. The guests moved through to the next room where a dance floor was set up. An enthusiastic DJ welcomed them all in and summoned the bride and groom to the centre.

"Oh, look, their first dance," Maddy said to her husband as he rejoined her looking relieved, poor man.

Hannah smiled to herself as Rachael and Ben took the floor. This was not going to be the romantic waltz Maddy would be expecting. Sure enough, within seconds, the first soft notes moved into the pounding beat of the *hora* music. Suddenly the floor was swamped with people. The bride and groom were whisked into separate circles, the men linked around Ben, the women around Rachael as the two circles spun faster and faster alongside each other.

Hannah stepped in, clasping someone's waist, feeling someone else clasp her own as they spun, all hair and perfume and laughter around the special girl of the day. Hannah breathed in the scent of her childhood and felt something build inside her — joy! Was it joy? It was something close to it, certainly.

Next moment, the men were breaking through, whisking Rachel up on to a chair and twirling her up and off to parade with her husband above the rest of them. Hannah saw Rachael reach out, clasp Ben's hands, hold his gaze before they were off again in a huge swirl of love.

Then suddenly there were new hands on her waist. She turned and found herself only centimetres from Tom. His dark brown eyes were staring down into hers.

"That could have been us," he said quietly.

She nodded, suddenly overwhelmed by the thought, struggling to remember why she'd resisted so petulantly, so stubbornly.

"But you were right," he went on, "we were too young. We'd have smashed that glass!"

Hannah gulped, not at all sure that this was what she wanted to hear. Tom's arms were still around her and they felt so good, so safe, as if they were holding her in an amazing stillness against him as the rest of the wedding party whirled madly around them.

Yet he was saying they hadn't been right for each other — wasn't he?

"Do you think so?" she asked in a small voice.

"I do."

Hannah felt disappointment lurch inside her and looked downwards abruptly, biting her lip. But Tom hadn't finished.

"We wouldn't have made it together — then. Now, though, Hannah, *now* we might stand a better chance."

Her head went up once more. She met his eyes and, with a tiny gasp, she saw love still flickering in them. It was a faint light but it held promise — so much promise.

"What do you think?" he asked softly.

Hannah swallowed hard.

"I think," she replied tentatively, "that we're certainly worth a second chance."

Tom gave a slow smile and, as his lips dipped deliciously towards her, she couldn't help thinking of the bridal canopy next door and of how maybe, at last, her dad would lead her towards it for her own special day.

For now, though, today was special enough, and lacing her hands around Tom's wonderfully familiar neck, she gave in to joy at last. ■

The Measure Of Life

by Gillian Bligh.

A POCKET watch!" Hugo looked at me across the dining table. "We can't buy you a pocket watch for your sixtieth birthday, Mother."

"Why not?" I asked indignantly. "That's what I would like."

"Well —" He shot his sister a "please help me

Illustration by Melvyn Warren-Smith.

out here" look. "For a start, it's a man's present; how many women do you know with a pocket watch?"

"None, actually. But that doesn't mean I shouldn't have one."

"It's not a very practical present, Mother," Amelia said, as if she was talking to someone who had suddenly taken leave of their senses. "Where would you keep it?"

They were obviously convinced I would not have an answer.

"I could buy a waistcoat," I said, only half serious. "Lots of women wear waistcoats; I was looking at some very attractive ones only yesterday. Or I could keep it in the side pocket of my handbag, or I could buy one of those pretty little rosewood stands and have it on the dresser beside your father's photograph."

"There, that's three options straight away."

"Father didn't like pocket watches."

"No, but I do."

The children had invited me for dinner at my daughter Amelia's house to discuss my forthcoming birthday and retirement. I'd suspected why as soon as Hugo rang me.

"Just we three, Mother," he had said enticingly. "It's ages since the three of us have had a meal together. We want to talk to you about something important."

So here we were — the three of us, enjoying our coffee and mints.

L ET'S go into the sitting-room," Amelia suggested, as if she thought a more comfortable chair might bring me to my senses.

"I don't know what all the fuss is about." I was genuinely baffled. "You're both fully aware of my interest in timepieces. You never showed surprise when your father bought me clocks, and you know I was overjoyed with the wristwatch you all bought me for my fiftieth."

They exchanged disappointed looks. Perhaps, I thought suddenly, they might think I was expecting an expensive watch?

Amelia cut in on my thoughts.

"Wouldn't you like something a little more feminine, Mother? Something that you could show off to your friends without them thinking you were a little . . ."

"Batty?" I suggested helpfully.

"Well, eccentric."

"They both mean the same thing, don't they?" I said flatly. "Anyway, pocket watches are very feminine. I've seen some very intricately decorated ones, and some have miniature paintings on them that . . ." This time *my* voice trailed off.

"Oh," I said quickly, "I don't want you to spend a fortune on an antique painted one. That would be much too expensive! You can get quite pretty gold-plated ones for around thirty pounds."

"You've obviously been studying the market," Hugo said suspiciously.

"Good heavens no, not recently. Your father and I often looked around antiques shops and jewellers. It was what we enjoyed doing," I said wistfully, as I brought his face to mind.

"Dad knew I liked clocks and watches. I don't know why. I just do."

"You've a house full of clocks, Mother," Hugo said exasperatedly. "You must spend an hour a week just winding them."

"One more wouldn't make much difference, then, would it?" I placed my coffee cup back in its saucer. The topic of conversation had produced an atmosphere, which made me slightly sad.

"Don't look so dejected," I said brightly. "I'm sure I can think of something you would approve of buying me. Or how about a surprise? You know my tastes so well that none of your presents are ever disappointing. That's it — surprise me!"

I beamed my best motherly smile at them and was pleased to see relief on their faces.

"It was a beautiful meal," I added. "Did I really teach you to cook that well?"

L ATER that evening I walked around my home proudly looking at my clock collection. As I went, I found myself fingering my gold wristwatch.

There was the cuckoo clock that used to intrigue me as a child when I visited my elderly uncle. No-one was more surprised than I was when he bequeathed it to me.

I smiled as I remembered him telling me that every night, at midnight, the cuckoo came right out of the clock and flew around the room. Well, it's nearly midnight now, I thought, watching the hands creep towards the top of the dial.

On the top of the china cabinet stood a rosewood and burr walnut mantel clock, a present from Robert in our better-off years. There was glass on all four sides of the timepiece. I watched as the cogs clicked around effortlessly before a little hammer made a pretty *ding!* on the bell at the top, proclaiming midnight.

Almost immediately Grandfather began chiming in the hall — a wonderfully full, deep, resonant Westminster chime that could be heard all over the house, strangely comforting if I woke in the night. In childhood, I used to listen for the mantel clock to chime as I lay in bed in the middle of the night. Things don't change much!

My eyes drifted down to the china cabinet. On the middle shelf was a miniature enamel clock decorated with pink rosebuds. It hadn't worked for years, but I liked it, and it brought back memories of my first love — the boy from two doors down the lane, who had given me the clock for Christmas, before moving with his family to Scotland. A few letters had passed between us but then he'd met a Scots lass . . .

Over the desk was the brass ship's clock in a ship's wheel. My Hugo had made it for me — he'd always been good at woodwork.

Beside the clock was a photograph of my grandfather — a young man in Naval uniform — with Grandma and their family. They'd all gone now. I kept in touch with some of their other grandchildren — my cousins.

From the dining-room came the sound of the little mahogany wall clock chiming. Slow as usual — I really must regulate it next time I wound it. I knew why I put it off each time; it was because I liked to hear all the clocks chime individually rather than in unison.

No, perhaps I'd leave it after all.

I wandered through and studied the little clock, which had a glass front through which you could see the hammers as they chimed the quarter hours. I liked to watch them.

It was a soft chime, Westminster like the Grandfather, but much, much softer.

On the shelf on the opposite side of the room stood Grandma's domed walnut clock with tiny finials at the four corners and on top. I closed my eyes and saw it again on Grandma's mantelpiece — I could almost smell her famous steak and kidney pie wafting through from the kitchen . . .

BACK in the sitting-room, a sturdy brass carriage clock stood elegantly between the candlesticks on the mantelshelf. Four brass baubles travelled around one way, then silently changed direction and went the other way. As they moved around they caught the sun, sending little patterns of light all around the room — very relaxing to watch.

The children had bought us that one for our fortieth anniversary.

I switched off the lamp and went through to my bedroom. Passing through the hall, I stopped to admire Grandfather. His weights and pendulum shone. The regular tick and gently swaying pendulum were so relaxing. Who needed sleeping pills when you could sit on the bottom stair and listen to Grandfather for ten minutes? Much, much more effective.

I took off my watch and returned it to the presentation box, as I did every night.

I looked at the small china clock beside the bed. Amelia had bought it for me one Christmas after I had admired it on one of our rare days out together. It's very pretty, a white background decorated with all sorts of things from nature — a pale blue bird's egg, a feather, a bee, a primrose . . .

I picked it up and held it in my hand. It was almost like picking Amelia up and holding her in my arms as a baby — I felt so close to her. Twelve-thirty, the little clock told me — I'm late tonight. I don't like going to bed late, or getting up late. I like to make good use of my time.

* * * *

Three months later, the phone was ringing as I opened the front door.

"Hello?" I said happily, expecting Amelia or Hugo.

"Is that Maisie?" a vaguely familiar voice asked.

"Yes?"

"Cousin Reg. I'm in your area, can I call round?"

"Yes, yes, of course! I'll put the kettle on."

Cousin Reg! I hadn't seen him in thirty years.

Reg and I spent two hours catching up on family news.

"You haven't changed much, Maisie."

"Haven't I?"

"Can you remember Grandad?" he asked.

Somewhere in the deep recesses of my mind was a hazy memory of a tall, kind man with a big beard.

"Vaguely," I answered. "I wasn't very old when he died."

"I can see you now, sitting on his knee being entertained by his pocket watch."

I stared at Reg.

"His pocket watch?"

"Yes, he had a beautiful gold pocket watch, very ornate, much bigger than the ones you see today. First he'd open the front and show you the time. 'Time and tide wait for no man, Maisie,' he'd say. 'Make good use of your time, don't waste any.'

"Then he'd hold the watch to your ear to let you hear the ticking. After a while he'd turn the watch over and open the back where you could see all the little cogs turning. You were fascinated, Maisie.

"Yes, I can see you now. You loved your grandad, and you also loved his pocket watch . . ."

Tears came to my eyes as I looked across at the dresser, the photograph of Robert, and the rosewood stand holding my sixtieth birthday present — a lovely gold pocket watch. ■

And Flossie

ISN'T it strange how sometimes the past comes strolling back, collides with the present, and makes our future unfold in ways we would never have considered? Who would have thought that opening an old photograph album could have such far-reaching consequences?

The signpost said *left for Frinscombe Harbour, right for Frinscombe Point*. I flicked the indicator right and drove up the hill. It was nearer to sixty years than fifty since I'd walked up from the harbour to Frinscombe Point with my parents and sister.

Now there was a small car park set discreetly into the side of the hill. I got out and walked the last fifty yards to the top.

Nothing had changed. The breeze rattled in up here, and the late September sun gilded the wide sweep of the shallow West Bay where the little waves pootled in. The houses and small hotels were painted in fresh, clean pastels, the old harbour was busy with boats and the smaller East Bay below my feet was a small child's delight of boulders and rock pools, every one with its own treasures just waiting to be discovered.

I was startled. It should have changed. Was Frinscombe-on-Sea some sort of Brigadoon?

My thoughts were disturbed by a brown and white spaniel bounding up to me and woofing.

"Hello, baby. Where did you come from?"

"She did her usual trick and beat me up the hill," said a slightly out of breath, greying male head from just below the top of the slope. "Flossie, come here. No, Flossie."

But it was too late, Flossie had put her paws up on me, and I had

Came, Too

by Catherine M. Hicks.

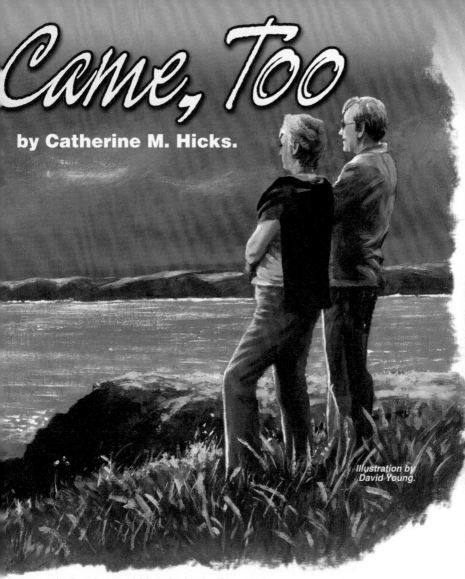

Illustration by David Young.

succumbed and was rubbing the back of her neck.

"Don't worry about it. I have . . . had a dog. And the grandchildren are even worse."

"Sorry," he said as he emerged and stopped to get his breath.

I glanced up at him. His was a pleasant enough face, and it belonged to my generation. He had nice brown eyes, a few lines, but they looked mostly due to laughter and not sour discontent.

His hair had, I think, been mid-brown but was now well speckled with grey, and worn rather longer than is fashionable for young men. He pushed it

59

back from his face and I did a double take. I knew that face. Then the brisk breeze blew it about again and I didn't.

"Flossie, come here."

"Go back to Dad, Flossie."

She ignored me and nudged me to continue rubbing her neck. A sudden gust of wind made me take a step back.

"Flossie, don't push the lady."

"Flossie is innocent, it was the breeze. I'd forgotten how bracing it is up here."

"You're a regular visitor to Frinscombe, then?" he said, coming over and clipping Flossie's lead on. She gave him a baleful look and sat down.

"I haven't been since I was a small child."

"About twenty years ago?"

"Flatterer," I said with a laugh. "It's nearer twenty-five."

"Still a good view, though. Have you walked up from the harbour?"

"No, I've just arrived. I'm parked down the hill a bit."

"Watch out for the one-way system in the village."

He ran through the worst of it and we chatted for a few minutes before Flossie woofed and tried to bound forward. A mongrel and an old black Lab were coming towards us, clearly friends of Flossie. We parted with a casual, "See you around."

THE Harbour View hotel provided me with a nice, large, clean room with a small shower-room and a comfortable squashy armchair by the window with a view over the promenade. I had dinner in the hotel, a nice chat with the owner about good walks in the area, sponged out the Flossie paw marks I hadn't noticed earlier on my jacket and had an early night.

I took a brisk walk along the prom before breakfast the next day and saw Flossie and her man approaching. With the breeze in his face and his hair blown back, I again had the fleeting impression that I knew him.

Flossie put her paws up for me to rub her neck. Fortunately this morning they were clean. We chatted for a few minutes about this and that before Flossie spotted a cairn terrier.

"Do you know there's a good market in Waverly today?" the man said.

" Where is Waverly? Is it far?"

"About four miles inland."

"I can't resist a market. I'll have a look at it this morning."

Guessing correctly that parking would be next to impossible in Waverly, I caught the bus after breakfast with the intention of walking back. Flossie's man was right — it was a good market. I bought a caramel-coloured sweater and some local honey and fudge before I was found at a second-hand book stall.

"Are you a bibliophile as well?" Flossie's man asked.

"I'm afraid so. No, Flossie, no fudge. It's not good for you." She had her nose in my bag. I slung it over my shoulder out of her reach.

"Try Carter's on the High Street in Frinscombe."

"No, really, I shouldn't," I said, glancing at the small pile I had already chosen. "It's going to be one of the hardest parts of downsizing. I have so many."

"I know. It's sensible, but so difficult. I don't know where they come from. I keep meaning to have a clear out, but never get round to it."

"I'm rattling round my house like a pea in a drum on my own. And there are so many diversions when you start. That's why I'm in Frinscombe. I found some holiday snaps from when I was a small child, and on an impulse rang up the tourist board and they booked me a hotel here."

"Can I do my part for promoting the local tourist industry and ask you to join Flossie and me at the Church Inn for lunch?" he said rather quickly.

I looked down at my books to give myself time to think. It was so long since I'd been invited anywhere that I wasn't sure what to say. I looked up into his steady brown eyes and noticed that he seemed nervous. He was biting his lip.

"In a while, that is. It's a bit early for lunch," he added.

"Yes. Yes, please. That would be very nice."

I'm sure it wasn't the warmth of the September sun on my face. I think I blushed. I felt like a teenager, not a granny.

"Great. I'm Michael Chiltern."

"Sharon Philips."

MICHAEL and Flossie were clearly well known at the Church Inn, as he ordered her a lamb chop, and when it came he cut it up and put it in a blue melamine bowl that he produced from his backpack. She went to sleep with her head on my feet when she had licked the bowl clean inside and out twice over.

Perhaps it was the sleeping dog on my feet which made me feel at home. Perhaps it was due to Michael's slightly anxious look, which matched my own feelings, when he had asked me to lunch. Either way I had a really comfortable hour with the two of them.

Michael and Flossie had driven over as he had stuff to collect for the hotel where he worked part-time. He offered to drop my shopping at my hotel, leaving me unencumbered for the walk back to Frinscombe.

Perhaps it was the holiday mood I was in, or perhaps it was all the old memories that were being stirred up by starting to clear out the clutter that had accumulated over the years but, as I strolled back to Frinscombe, my mind wandered back through the years. Oddly enough, though, my memories weren't of the holidays I'd had in Frinscombe, but of being a teenager.

I remembered going to the pictures and dances with my friends Jenny and May. Jenny and I were the shy, quiet ones. May always had boys buzzing around her.

I recalled the music we listened to — and my dad's derisive remarks about it. May's brother, Jon, was in a group, and my parents were horrified when I told them that we had been to a concert. I was at once forbidden to go to any more.

But I went to one more. Jon, of course, knew people in other bands and said he could get us backstage to meet . . .

What was the name of the group?

And their handsome lead singer?

After all these years I couldn't remember. But I did remember how excited I'd been forty-odd years ago. I laughed and gave my attention to the scenery in the hope that the name would come back if I didn't press too hard. But it didn't and the walk was so spectacular that it slipped to the back of my mind.

It didn't entirely disappear, though, and at odd moments the question would return.

What was that band called?

I'D booked three nights at the Harbour View hotel with the intention of coming home if the weather was bad or I didn't like Frinscombe, or staying a few more days if the weather was fair and I was enjoying myself.

I walked all round the town and pottered about in the shops, without any definite purchase in mind. I succumbed to the lure of Carter's book store and bought more than I should have.

I walked over the cliffs and explored the bays and coves and beaches. I stopped for coffee, or lunch or afternoon tea when and where I fancied. In short I had full command of my time and I loved it. I seemed to have had so little of that these last few years.

I'd retired early to take care of Alan when he became ill. And afterwards it had seemed foolish to try to go back to work at my age, when there were so many small grandchildren to be looked after for at least part of the day.

I hadn't even been on holiday on my own. I'd been away two or three times a year with one or another family group.

Don't get me wrong: I love all eight grandchildren and their half-a-dozen parents, but it was nice to be alone, to do what I wanted and not to have to keep up the high concentration levels needed to deal with small children.

To start to remember who Sharon Philips was in her own right, not just as a mother, a mother-in-law and a granny.

I was also putting off starting to clear some of the accumulation of years from the house before I put it on the market. It was miles too big for me on my own, and the garden was massive and becoming unruly. But it was a big job and everything stirred up memories.

And it was . . . interesting to keep bumping into Michael and Flossie. I missed my old Oscar and found it very pleasant to have Flossie go to sleep on my feet as Michael and I chatted and, yes, he joined me for some of the afternoon teas and morning coffees.

Michael was a widower with two daughters, the elder of whom had taken

Turlough Museum, Co. Mayo, Ireland

WHAT a nice reminder to see your stunning picture of Turlough Museum. I was on a coach tour there, and can tell you that this National Folk Life collection is a sight to see. Through clothing, tools, furniture etc. they gave us a glimpse of a way of life which is nearly gone. They hold regular demonstrations of basket weaving and spinning, as well as butter-making. We also enjoyed visiting the very nice café and shop!

— *M.H., Aberdeen.*

J. CAMPBELL KERR.

over the running of his hotel with her husband. He was still involved with the hotel business and was grandfather to twin baby girls.

I decided that another three days in Frinscombe would be nice. I still couldn't place who it was that Michael reminded me of when his hair was taken back, usually by a gust of wind. I dismissed it as a passing resemblance to some actor or sportsman or newsreader. He wasn't like anyone I knew.

Nor had the name of the group I had secretly defied my parents to go to see come back. Jon had been as good as his word and had taken the three of us backstage to meet his friends in this group whose name eluded me after all these years.

I had been thrilled to be backstage, with all its controlled chaos, and I'd had about ninety seconds' conversation with their handsome lead singer, whatever his name was. Then an older woman (probably about eighteen or nineteen) had put her hand on his arm. He had turned and smiled, said goodbye to me and gone off with her.

How vital it had seemed then. How tiresomely trivial it was, now that I had forgotten all the names.

ON my fourth evening in Frinscombe I decided to treat myself to dinner at the Frinscombe Bay hotel, a large, white, recently refurbished Art Deco building at the very western end of the bay. I was seated and had ordered my meal before I saw Michael at a table across the restaurant, with a beautiful young woman.

I ate my seafood salad with a growing feeling of betrayal. We had taken walks together. We had moved on from the casual chat of fellow dog-walkers. I had thought I was beginning to get to know him. He had seemed interested in me.

The fact that he was dining with a lovely young woman in an expensive restaurant, after having had tea with me in a cliff-top hut that same afternoon and not mentioning it, showed how wrong I was.

He was seated with his back to me and was involved in animated conversation with the young woman. The waiter had taken my plate away when Michael turned around, scanned the restaurant, saw me and smiled.

He turned back to his companion, spoke briefly, got up and came across to me. I felt myself blush, but I wasn't going to make a scene.

"Sharon, I didn't know you were dining here tonight. Won't you come and join us?"

"Thank you, no. I should make an uncomfortable third."

"Not a bit of it. I'd like you to meet Susannah. She'd arrived home from university when I got back from our walk this afternoon."

"Susannah? Your daughter?"

"Yes." Michael smiled.

"Please come and join us, Mrs Philips," Susannah said, standing just behind her father. "Dad's been telling me all about you."

He didn't seem embarrassed by this revelation, so we had the second half of our meals together. Susannah was a pretty, slender, fair-haired girl who apparently took after her mother.

IT was dark by the time we left the hotel and Michael suggested that, as we had to pass his hotel to get to mine, I come in for coffee and then he would walk me back. I agreed, but our plans were thwarted when his elder daughter waylaid us and insisted we come up to their flat.

I can only assume that Susannah had made a quick call to her sister, as there was no other reason for her to have been fiddling with tourist board leaflets in the foyer at that time of the evening.

Carol was dark, and with her hair swept up in a pony tail, was every inch her father's daughter. Her husband, Carl, joined us in their flat a few minutes later and I knew I was being inspected.

One of the twins started to cry.

"Charlotte," Carl said. "She wants you to sing to her, Dad."

Michael went out, and a few moments later I heard him start with "Twinkle, Twinkle, Little Star". It was hardly a novelty and he gave it no unconventional twist. He was just singing it quietly to his baby granddaughter.

A memory stirred, but I concentrated on my coffee and the conversation in the room . . . and the fact that I had felt a pang of jealousy when I had seen Michael with his daughter and leaped to the wrong conclusion.

I stayed a polite half hour before I said I must be going. Michael got up to walk me back, then collected Flossie from his flat.

At the front door of the hotel Michael made to turn left.

"Let's walk down the promenade. It's a nice evening."

Only the gentle lapping waves broke the silence for a little while.

"So, tell me, Michael," I said at last, "when did you give up being Angel Lee, and do you still see much of the Heavenly Rock Band?"

Michael was silent for a second.

"What?"

"Forty-odd years ago you were Angel Lee and your backing band was the Heavenly Rock Band."

"Yes." He stopped walking. "Who told you?"

"Nobody told me. I remembered. The first time I saw you I thought you reminded me of someone. Tonight I saw Carol, and I heard you singing to the baby. It came back to me."

"After all these years," he said, shaking his head.

"Michael, I had a teenage crush on you."

"On me?"

"Yes." I explained about Jon getting us backstage.

"I'm sorry. I don't remember. There were always so many people about."

"When I was fifteen I would have been dreadfully hurt that you didn't remember me. Now I understand perfectly."

Michael nodded slowly. We walked on a little way in silence and found ourselves at the harbour.

"Are you cold?" he asked.

"No."

"Let's sit for a while."

INSTEAD of making for a nearby bench he lifted me up on to the harbour wall, put Flossie up beside me and I put my arm around her before he sprang up beside me.

"You've met the drummer, of course."

"I have?"

"Peter Carter, at the bookshop."

Chubby, amiable, thinning grey hair and half-moon glasses.

"Dan, the bass guitarist, lives near Norwich and he's recently retired from a building society. Clark, the lead guitarist, moved to Canada years ago. Something to do with timber."

I took a minute to absorb this information.

"So, what happened? What went wrong? How come the Heavenly Rock Band turned into lumberjacks and building society managers?"

"Nothing went wrong. We gave it up. Pete was married. Anne and I were engaged. Dan was serious about a girl. It was always about the music for us, not the fame and the money.

"The music scene was beginning to change. We weren't too keen to change with it. Who knows what might have happened if we'd stayed together? Perhaps we could all have become obscenely rich, who knows?"

"That doesn't sound like it appeals much."

"Well, I occasionally fantasise about the obscenely rich part. But I'd rather have had the years with Anne and the girls. We thought it better to come back here and take over my parents' hotel."

Flossie snuggled up on to my lap.

"How much longer are you going to be in Frinscombe?"

"I've booked in for another three days."

"But your home is only, what, eighty-five, ninety miles away?" His gaze held mine, hesitant and hopeful.

"About that."

"That's not really so far."

"Not really."

"But, before you go back and I have to keep driving over to see you, how about a day at Feversham Castle Gardens tomorrow?"

"Can Flossie come as well?"

"She can."

"In that case, I'd love to." ■

On The Right Track...

by Marina Livingston.

Illustration
by David Axtell.

I SWALLOWED the aspirin as the noise from the spare room reached a crescendo. From what I could hear, I realised that Matthew had won again — which wouldn't have pleased Drew and Steven one little bit. Just as well their dad was present to stop anyone coming to blows.

Who was I kidding? A lot of the noise was coming from him, not his sons.

Sitting down at the kitchen table, I thought back to when my Saturday afternoons were a haven of peace, just knowing Ian was off with the boys and wouldn't be back till early evening. I'd get back from town with a copy of my favourite magazine and a bar of milk chocolate, and curl up in front of the fire for a few hours. Bliss!

They were all keen hill-walkers, so most Saturdays saw them out in the fresh air from early morning. During the winter, they'd abandon the hills and stand on the terracing yelling support for their team. If I ever regretted having three sons and no daughters, having Saturdays to myself definitely made up for it.

Another yell from upstairs made me jump. But what was the point of complaining? It was all my own fault and I knew it.

*   *   *   *

It all started last month when Donna from next door asked if I could help out with another fund-raising event for the local school. This time it was a car boot sale. I could never see the attraction. I remember when they were simply called jumble sales. Setting up and standing around in a field rather than a draughty church hall didn't change that.

But I wanted to offer my support because it's a nice little school and, like others, it's short of money.

To be honest, I don't think they do too badly. At least they have plenty of room for the kiddies to run about, and beautiful playing fields. And besides, I was a pupil there myself, so I'll always have a soft spot for it. But I digress; to get back to the car boot sale, Donna asked me if I could help to collect some of the things being donated by people who couldn't attend.

This would involve using Ian's van, which he wasn't too happy about. It meant that, every night after work, he had to unload all his tools and give the van a good sweeping out. You can guess how much more annoyed he got when I sprained my ankle the very first night, and for the remaining four nights he had to come with me to drive me around.

That's why, when something happened to cheer him up, I encouraged him. It seemed a small price to pay and, at the time, I didn't realise that the true cost would be the loss of my precious Saturday afternoons.

Mr Anderson had cleared out his attic and helped Ian to carry the stuff to the van, while I sat in the passenger seat chatting to his wife, who'd come out to say hello and commiserate about my dodgy ankle. She had big plans for their attic, now that all the junk had gone.

I'd always fancied having our own attic converted, so I was interested in what she had to say — she'd done her homework, and knew exactly which builders she was getting in. I was about to start taking notes when I realised the sighing had begun again.

Ian, loading over, had rejoined me and was huffing and puffing like a steam engine in his anxiety to end our conversation so we could leave.

I said my goodbyes, and accepted the invitation to pop round when they had the job finished — which pleased me no end. If the builders turned out to be dodgy, at least it wouldn't be my attic that suffered for it.

S O off we went and I was surprised when, just a few streets away, Ian pulled over.

"Rose, come and see this." He chortled.

I hobbled round to the back of the van and peered inside. Nothing immediately caught my attention, so I watched as Ian rearranged a few things, then wrestled a large box from the depths. I looked at it blankly — an absence of brothers during my formative years meant that whatever had made Ian so happy meant nothing to me.

I looked again, taking in the rather tatty box, ripped at the corners. A colourful picture on the lid showed sleek racing cars hurtling around a track; artistic licence, I'm afraid. When Ian pulled off the lid, all I could see were pieces of black plastic and a few tiny cars.

"Isn't it brilliant?" he said, stroking one of the cars. "I had one just like this as a lad." Then he looked thoughtful. "I wonder what happened to it?" he mused.

Knowing my father-in-law, I assumed the toy had been thrown away once Ian outgrew it. He wasn't much of a hoarder, unlike his son.

When we got home, Ian unloaded the van, leaving almost everything in the shed alongside the rest of the stuff we'd collected that week. I say "almost everything" because the box with the racing cars was brought straight into the house.

"I'm just going to check it's all there," he said, not meeting my eyes. "We can't really sell it with bits missing."

I sat down to phone my sister, and a few minutes later heard the unmistakable sound of furniture being moved around. Even Margo could hear it.

"What on earth's going on in your house, Rose?" she said, and I explained about Ian taking the box upstairs.

"And is he rearranging the furniture? Just to check there are no pieces missing?" Margo was baffled.

"I don't know," I said, equally mystified. "Look, I'll call you tomorrow. I want to go and see what he's up to."

I hung up to the sound of Margo's laughter, and hopped across the sitting-room and into the hall, stopping at the bottom of the stairs.

"Ian?"

There was no reply.

It took a few minutes for me to get upstairs, but I was soon standing at the door of the spare room looking at the furniture, now pushed aside and arranged around the walls. The rug, which had lain on the polished floor next to the bed, had been rolled up untidily and was propped against the wardrobe.

My husband was on his hands and knees, fitting one piece of black plastic on to another.

"Oh, it's the track!" I said, enlightenment dawning with each satisfying click as the "road" began to take shape. Quite a boring shape, I have to say. A simple circle, that's all. But Ian looked as if he'd just found a cure for the common cold. He stood up, proudly surveying the shiny plastic, before hunkering down again to fiddle with the power supply. I left him to it, and hopped back downstairs to watch television.

By bedtime, he'd got the cars in working order and, beaming, offered me first go. I admit, it was a little bit thrilling to watch my car speeding round the track, though it took a bit of practice to avoid having it fly off and slide across the room every now and again.

Ten minutes was enough, though, and I lost interest and went to bed.

The following night, the evening before the car boot sale, Ian came home carrying a large bag.

Moon-daisy Meadow

*I*N moon-daisy meadow
I played as a child,
In moon-daisy meadow
The flowers grew wild,
And summer days lingered
On sweet scented air,
The humming of insects
As soft as a prayer.
And there, on my back,
I would lie in the grass
And sleepily watch
As the clouds drifted past,
And all the world gleamed
In a warm, hazy glow,
In moon-daisy meadow
So long, long ago.

— *Maggie Ingall.*

"The track was just a bit small," he said defensively. "But just look what I found in Mullets, that second-hand shop behind the high street!"

He would have had no reason at all to be anywhere near the high street today, so I immediately knew that he'd made a special trip — and, in all probability, had phoned first to see if they had the item he wanted. I didn't say any of this, though. I've learned when to keep my own counsel.

He disappeared upstairs with the bag, and I heard the sound of furniture moving again. There goes the bed, I thought, and I was right. When I went up later, the bed, previously in a prominent position, had been pushed sideways against the window.

And the racing track was now three times its original size.

Ian was over the moon.

"I remembered you used to be able to buy extra track. Wasn't it good luck that Mullets had this? And it was going for a song!"

"Er . . . Ian . . ." I began. "You do know you can't keep it, don't you? It has to be sold for the school funds."

"Don't worry, pet," he said, greedily eyeing the massive display. "It *is* sold! To me!" And he named a sum which I knew would be eagerly accepted by whoever was doing the pricing. True to his word, he paid me in cash right there and then.

What could I say?

I stayed a while and watched the little cars whizzing around, and listening to Ian's monologue about how kids nowadays don't know how to have fun,

Maggie Ingall.

with their silly computer games and mobile phones and so on. I went back downstairs and half an hour later he joined me. I could tell he was getting bored playing by himself, and was waiting for our sons.

The minute they walked through the door, he hustled them upstairs and that was the last I saw of them for two hours.

I still didn't see the signs. I thought the novelty would soon wear off, the track would be packed up and put in the box, and there it would stay until it was our turn to clear our attic and get it ready to be turned into another room.

But it wasn't to be. Every Saturday since then, my boys had congregated in the spare room to the sounds of whoops and cheers. My only purpose during this time was when one or another of them came downstairs.

"Mum, I'm starving!"

This was my cue to start grilling bacon and filling rolls for my son to take upstairs to share with his father and brothers.

I was in the kitchen, grilling yet more bacon, when the back door opened and my saviours walked in. I'd never been so happy to see the three of them, as they gathered round me for a hug, all the time sympathising about the loss of the one day I looked forward to most all week.

"Don't worry," they said. "We'll sort it out."

AND they did. Within minutes, all my boys were lined up in the kitchen being told, in no uncertain terms, that they were being very selfish. A short time later, the black plastic track was dismantled and stowed away, and my spare room was back to normal. You'd hardly have known they'd been there; every stick of furniture was restored to its rightful place.

I looked at them, standing there shame-faced. My sixty-year-old husband, and my three sons, none of whom would ever see thirty again. And my three beautiful daughters-in-law, bless every one of them. We couldn't stay angry for long, though, and as they all moved *en masse* through the back door, I heard my youngest, Steven, speaking.

"We can set it up in my garage," he was saying eagerly. "It won't do the car any harm to stay outside for a while . . ."

And my three girls shook their heads wearily and laughed, but said no more. They, too, knew that this was another one of those times when it's best to keep quiet.

I got my Saturday afternoons back, and that's the important thing. ■

71

"THERE'S a tent in your back garden, Grandad," Jodie said. "A pink one."

"Is there really?" Bob said, looking suitably shocked. "A pink tent, you say? You'd better show me."

Jodie took his hand and led him to the back door.

"Well, my word," he said. "There *is* a tent in my back garden. Now how did that get there?"

Jodie giggled.

"You put it there, Grandad," she said. "I know you did."

"Did I?" He laughed, but he'd been sussed.

"Can I get in it, Grandad?" Jodie asked.

"It's yours." Bob grinned. "You can do what you like with it."

He watched her run down the garden with his collie, Cass, in hot pursuit. The pair of them disappeared through the flap.

"Dad, I thought I told you . . ." Shirley began in her usual exasperated tones.

"No tent," he said, recalling their words of just a few days ago. "That's right, you did. Dearie me, I must have forgotten."

"Oh, Dad, you shouldn't spoil Jodie like that. She doesn't need all these things

by Teresa Ashby.

you keep buying for her. And that's no ordinary tent, is it? It's even got windows!"

Bob turned his back to her and filled the kettle. There were times when Shirley was so like her mother that if they were both in the room at the same time it would be hard to tell one from the other.

AUDREY used to moan at him when Shirley was little, always telling him off for spoiling her.

He'd come home from sea and Shirley would run into his arms.

"What have you got for me, Daddy?" she'd cry and he'd dig around in his bag until he found some treat or other. It was never anything expensive, just a Belgian chocolate bar or a tiny doll from Greece, though once he'd brought her a gold silk embroidered dressing-gown from Japan. She'd worn it until it had fallen apart.

"You shouldn't spoil her," Audrey used to say. But he could never see why not. Sometimes he was away for weeks on end and the thought of his little girl waiting at home kept him going.

"It's only a tent," he muttered now. "It wasn't expensive."

"Yes, it was, but that's not the point, Dad," Shirley said. "She only has to say she likes something and the next week you've bought it for her. She's got to learn that she can't have everything she wants."

"She's only five," Bob said. "And she's my only grandchild."

Jodie burst back in the kitchen again, face wreathed with smiles. It did Bob's heart good to see her so happy.

"Like it, pumpkin?" Bob said.

"I love it, Grandad. Thank you for buying it for me," Jodie cried and flung her arms round him. He lifted her up and cuddled her tight. He'd never thought it was possible to love another child as much as he'd loved Shirley, but he did. He loved Jodie so much that it hurt.

He set her down and gave Shirley an I-told-you-so look.

Illustration
by Sally
Rowe.

73

"Come and see my tent, Mummy," Jodie said and grasped Shirley's hand. "It's beautiful. It's like a palace."

"I never had a tent," Shirley muttered, but she was smiling. "I had to make do with Gran's old candlewick bedspread draped over the washing line and held in place with stones."

Bob laughed as he watched his two girls walking down the garden. They were so alike with their straight fair hair and summer-blue eyes.

A S he got cups out of the cupboard, his smile faded. It was true what Shirley said, he thought, she *had* had to make do a lot of the time. Make do and go without. He could count on the fingers of one hand the times he'd really been able to spoil her.

He'd wanted to buy Shirley a tent, but Audrey had put her foot down.

"What does a little girl want a tent for?" she said. "None of her friends has one. It's just a waste of money. If you're in the mood for splashing out, we've an electric bill that needs paying. I had the red reminder today."

It was the same when Shirley wanted a doll's-house. Her friend, Tricia, had a veritable doll's mansion, beautifully furnished with a working shower and little cupboards with opening drawers and doors. Tricia's parents had shown it to Bob when he went to collect Shirley from a party at their house.

"That must have cost a fortune," Bob said.

"It did, too," Tricia's father said, biting down on his pipe and looking pleased with himself. "But she's worth it."

Shirley was worth it, too, but there was no way Bob and Audrey could afford such a thing.

"I'd love a doll's-house for my birthday, Daddy," she'd said as they walked home.

"Well, perhaps . . ."

He was no expert, but he was willing, and he built a house, working quietly in the attic when he was on leave so that Shirley wouldn't see what he was up to. He made it so that the whole front of the house opened like a door — and unlike Tricia's doll's-house, Bob's had a proper staircase.

He decorated each room with different patterned paper and when it was finished, he started on the furniture. That was a fiddly business, especially in the dim light from the solitary bulb in the attic.

It was a real labour of love and it took him months to finish — just in time for Shirley's birthday. It was only when he looked at the finished article that he realised he'd built a replica of the house he grew up in. It looked a little old-fashioned even to his eyes.

The day before her birthday, while Shirley was at school, he carried the doll's-house carefully down the ladder. In the cold light of day, he could see all its many flaws.

The roof was wonky and so was the chimney. The brick-patterned paper

he'd stuck to the outside was slightly skew-whiff and the front of the house didn't fit quite flush.

"The furniture is lovely," Audrey said, clearly struggling to find something positive to say. "Look at the gloss on that wardrobe, and I love the little handles. You are clever, Bob."

But his heart sank. He could see the house with fresh eyes and he knew that Shirley would be disappointed.

"I can't give it to her," he murmured. "It's dreadful."

He carried the doll's-house back up to the attic where it would stay until he had time to break it up and put it in the bin. Before he went back down the ladder, he draped Gran's old candlewick bedspread over the top so he didn't have to look at it any more.

"We've time to get to the toy shop in town if we hurry," he said. "There must be something there we can afford. Perhaps we'll be able to pay for it a bit a week."

There was. It wasn't quite a mansion like Tricia's, but it was a neat little house with four rooms and flowers painted on the front wall. And the plastic furniture that came with it was just the thing.

HEY, sleepyhead." Audrey's voice cut into his thoughts. "You're miles away. Is that a kettle and a tea-bag I see before me or is it a mirage?"

"You're back." Bob hugged her. "I'll finish making the tea."

He reached for an extra mug.

"What was the hug for?" Audrey laughed. "I've only been shopping. Shirley's car is outside — where are they?"

"In the tent," Bob said.

"Oh, you put it up." Audrey dumped her shopping bags on the kitchen table and looked out of the window. "Does she like it?"

"Loves it," Bob said.

Hearing Audrey's voice, Shirley and Jodie emerged from the tent. Cass ran ahead of them barking a greeting.

"Hiya, Mum," Shirley said, giving her mother a kiss.

"Hello, Nanna," Jodie said. "Have you seen my tent?"

"It looks wonderful," Audrey said. "I'll come and have a proper look later. Right now I need a cuppa."

Bob got on with making the tea while Shirley drew Audrey to one side.

"Mum, you've got to stop him buying things for Jodie," she said.

"It's only a tent," Audrey said. "They were doing a special on them at the supermarket. It wasn't expensive. Anyway, forget the tent for a minute." Audrey rustled through her bags. "I saw this and couldn't resist it."

She pulled out a crimson cyclamen.

"I know how you love them," she said, handing it to her daughter. "And I got a little picnic set for Jodie to use in her tent."

Shirley looked pleased, but at the same time dismayed.

"You don't have to do this," she said.

"I know we don't." Audrey cast an anxious look at Bob. "We like to."

"Silly old sausages." Shirley hugged them both. "What would I do without you? I just wish you'd spend your money on yourselves for a change."

They left Bob in the kitchen and went out to look at the tent.

"That reminds me, Mum," Shirley said. "Remember my makeshift tent? Have you still got Gran's old candlewick bedspread?"

"Almost certainly." Audrey smiled. "It's probably up in the attic. I haven't been up there for donkey's years."

"Would it be all right if I went up and had a look for it? I thought if I gave it a good wash I could use it."

"Yes, if you want to. I bet it's dusty up there, though."

"Can I go in the attic, too?" Jodie asked.

"Yes, as long as you're careful," Shirley said. "I'm looking for a big pink blanket. You can help me."

B OB stood at the bottom of the loft ladder with Audrey and looked up through the hatch.

"What on earth are they doing up there?" he said.

"Looking for Gran's old bedspread," Audrey said.

"That old thing? Well, the last time I saw that, I —" He broke off. "Come down, Shirley!"

Her face appeared in the hatch above him, smeared with dust.

"What for? It's great up here, Dad," she said. "Like Aladdin's cave."

"Don't go rubbing any lamps, then." Audrey chuckled. "I haven't got room for a genie."

"I'd rather you came down," Bob said. "If you want a nice bedspread, we can buy you one . . ."

"Oh, Dad!" Shirley laughed.

"Found it . . . Oh, Mummy!" Jodie squealed.

"What is it?" Shirley vanished into the depths of the attic and Bob sighed deeply.

"Bob?" Audrey said.

Before he could explain, Shirley's face appeared above them again.

"Did you know there was a doll's-house up here? It's not my old one."

"Really?" Bob said and when she heard his attempt at a nonchalant tone it finally dawned on Audrey what they'd found up there.

"There's furniture, Mummy!" Jodie's voice drifted out. "Oh, it's so lovely."

"Lovely," Bob muttered. "Let's hope they don't want to bring it down into the daylight."

*   *   *   *

An hour later, Jodie was stretched out on her stomach playing with the doll's-house that now sat in the middle of the living-room floor.

"Surely you'd rather play in your tent?" Bob said. "On a nice day like today I would've thought you'd want to be outside."

"Leave her, Dad," Shirley said. "She's having fun."

There hadn't been any explanations as to where the doll's-house had come from and why it was in their attic and when Shirley had asked about it, her father had been very evasive, with a lot of muttering and shoulder shrugging.

When Audrey got up to make another cup of coffee, Shirley followed her into the kitchen.

"What's going on, Mum?" she said. "Why didn't I know about the doll's-house? Who put it there and what is it doing hidden away in the attic like that? I would have loved to have played with that."

"You would?" Audrey stared at her.

"Yes, it's beautiful. Not that I didn't love the one you and Dad gave me for my birthday, but you have to admit, that one is something special. Where did it come from? Who made it?"

"Your dad," Audrey said sheepishly.

"Dad? When? Why?"

"Oh, Shirley." Audrey bit her wobbling lip. "He made it for you, dear. He wanted you to have one as beautiful and posh as Tricia's and he worked so hard on it, but he wasn't at all pleased with the result and hid it away in the attic. I thought it had gone a long time ago. I didn't know it was still up there."

"Dad made that . . . for me?" Shirley whispered. She had never understood the feeling of a full heart until that moment. Now hers felt so full it might burst. "What about all those little bits of furniture?"

"Those, too." Audrey nodded.

Shirley tried to picture her dad with his big strong hands working so painstakingly on the little details. The cupboards all had little knobs and handles and tiny hinges held the doors in place.

She could just see him with his glasses perched on the end of his nose, getting hot up there in the attic, but ploughing on.

And he did it all for love.

"It just wasn't good enough for his little girl." Audrey sighed. "And you saw his face in there — he doesn't think it's good enough for his granddaughter, either."

"Right!" Shirley said and she marched back into the living-room.

"Has your mother told you?" Bob looked at her miserably. "You were never meant to see it, Shirley. I meant to smash it up and get rid of it, but I guess I forgot.

"It's awful, isn't it? I'll take it to the skip after you've gone. I'm just sorry Jodie's getting all mucky playing with the horrible old thing."

"Horrible old thing?" Shirley could barely get the words out. "Dad, it's the most beautiful thing I've ever seen in my life. Don't you dare take it to the skip!"

Shirley fell to her knees on the floor in front of Bob's chair.

"Dad, it's about time we got something straight," she said. "I would have loved the doll's-house — and because you made it for me, I would have loved it even more." She looked round at her mum.

"Don't either of you realise yet? I had the most wonderful childhood. All my memories are happy ones and I wouldn't trade a single minute for all the expensive gifts in the world. And Jodie feels the same. She loves coming here to see you — not to see what you've bought her, but to see *you*, the grandparents she adores."

Jodie had left the doll's-house and come over to stand beside her kneeling mother.

"I love the doll's-house, Grandad," she said. "Did you really make it?"

"Yes." Bob choked.

"It's perfect." Jodie grinned. "You are clever."

"See, you old silly." Shirley laughed. "I'm just glad we found it in the attic so it will get played with."

CAN the baby play with it, too?" Jodie asked.

"Baby?" Audrey caught her breath.

"Go on," Shirley said. "You can tell them, Jodie."

"I'm getting a baby brother or sister," Jodie announced proudly. "I wanted a rabbit, but Daddy says a baby will be more fun."

"And you'll bankrupt yourselves if you spoil two of them." Shirley laughed. "But you don't have to. All you have to do is be yourselves."

"You are my clever grandad," Jodie said, squeezing his neck and raining kisses all over his face. "And I love you *so* much."

Then she skipped across to Audrey, flinging her arms around her and cuddling her tight.

"I love you *so* much, too, Nanna," she said. "I love everybody! I'm the luckiest person in the whole world."

Not quite, Bob thought fondly, gazing round at his three unspoilt girls. That title was definitely reserved for him. ■

Step Back In Time

"War And Peace"

Courtesy of the
Royal Academy of Arts.

LEO TOLSTOY'S masterpiece, "War And Peace", was finally concluded in 1869 after being serialised for four years in "Russkii Vestnik" ("The Russian Herald"). "War And Peace" told the epic tale of five Russian families and the struggles they faced during the Napoleonic Era of early nineteenth-century Europe.

Although the book is set in Russia, much of the narration — including the opening sentence — is written in French. This cleverly reflects Russian society at the time, where many Russian aristocrats spoke French fluently. French was widely spoken within the European upper classes during the 1800s.

Although the book is regarded today as a novel, at the time of its publication Tolstoy broke so many traditional conventions of novels that his critics and even Tolstoy himself did not consider it to be one. Tolstoy, for example, had a huge collection of historical and fictional characters — the sheer volume of which allowed him to use characterisation to explore a number of themes.

One of the principal characters is Prince Andrei Bolkonski — a proud, handsome man; bored with high society life, he joins the Army in his search for glory. He is badly wounded and finds that everything he has devoted his life to has yielded nothing but profound emptiness.

One of the other main characters, Pierre Bezukhov, tries to find his meaning in life through philosophically questioning existence through a number of systems. However, he finds that enlightenment is not to be found in complex systems, but in the day-to-day trials of life.

The novel is not just a study of society. There is also a gripping love affair centred around Natasha, the heroine of the tale. Natasha falls in love with Andrei, yet is unaware of Pierre's admiration of her. Whom she will end up with leaves the reader guessing. The gaiety of Natasha's character, along with the love affair, lifts the narrative and brings the rest of the characters to life.

"War And Peace" is an epic study of not only history, but society and sociology, too. The world had never seen anything like it before, and many would struggle to think of such a comprehensive and important piece of work since. ∎

Every Picture Tells A Story

by Margaret Mounsdon.

Illustration by Diane Fawcett.

NAT stepped back to survey the centrepiece. It was fitting that it should be here for his first exhibition in his own studio.

Word had spread like wildfire and tickets had been snapped up the moment they were issued. Nat Taylor was a name to be reckoned with.

"A lovely touch, sir." His assistant hovered by his elbow. "Those old-fashioned prints are all the rage now and this picture speaks to you, doesn't it?"

Nat smiled. Old-fashioned? Perhaps it was, but his instinct told him it would draw the crowds as it had done many years ago — and his instinct had never let him down.

He smiled as he remembered the start of it all . . .

✳   ✳   ✳   ✳

"Er . . ." Nat knew he was making a fool of himself but he couldn't help it. He was looking into the bluest eyes he had ever seen and his vocal cords had temporarily frozen.

"Was there something?" she asked.

The girl did a good line in smiles, too, Nat thought as he continued to gape. Was that drumbeat really his heart?

There were one or two tuts of disapproval and remarks about "taking up the whole esplanade" as holidaymakers were forced to walk round them.

"I think we're in the way." The smile broadened and Nat caught a whiff of bluebells as she moved towards him.

Nat swallowed the blockage in his throat. Having plucked up the courage to speak to the girl, he'd now lost his nerve to see the thing through, which was unlike him.

"You're too full of yourself," his landlady always chided him when he was charming her into giving him an extra sausage at breakfast.

"Growing lad, need to keep up my strength," he would respond, adding, "No-one cooks a sausage like you, Mrs G."

But, so far, this week had been a disaster. It was only his second day in the job, and yesterday he had made so many mistakes Mr Simpkins had threatened to fire him unless he shaped up fast.

He wasn't supposed to spend his time smiling at beautiful young women in gingham dresses. He was supposed to be taking snapshots of the trippers and displaying them in the little kiosk by the amusement arcade.

The display was a great draw and nearly everyone stopped by to look and laugh and buy a holiday souvenir. But yesterday, Nat had left his lens cap on for the first half of the day. Then he'd taken some very interesting photographs of his right thumb and a fascinating shot of a pair of trousered boots outside a shop.

"It's the viewfinder," Nat tried to explain. "I'm sure I'll get the hang of it."

Mr Simpkins had not been amused.

"See that you do," he said. "I'm giving you one more chance. Now, it's a lovely sunny day. People are strolling about the place, the conditions are ideal. What are you waiting for?"

"Nothing, Mr Simpkins." Nat grabbed up his camera. "I'm on my way."

"And no more of these." Mr Simpkins thrust the disastrous photos at Nat.

After assuring Mr Simpkins there would be no repetition of yesterday's

81

mistakes, Nat had hared out the door in search of customers. He so wanted this job to be a success.

"We'll see how you get on," Mr Simpkins had said when he'd offered him the job on a temporary basis. "I'm not as young as I was and I need good, reliable help."

Nat would have taken the job with no pay. Cameras were the future and he wanted to be part of it. When Mr Simpkins retired he could see himself with a little studio and an assistant of his own.

THE second morning had been going well and Nat had snapped away happily at smiling grandmas, proud parents and sticky children waving candy floss and toffee apples at him.

He'd just been thinking about some lunch when this vision of loveliness had appeared from nowhere and totally distracted him from the job in hand.

"Do you want to take my picture? Is that it?" She pointed to the camera slung round Nat's neck.

"Yes." Remembering his manners, he tipped his boater at her.

"It's my lunch hour," she began. "I've only got thirty minutes."

"I could do you a special deal."

Where had that come from, Nat thought. He had no business offering special deals. Mr Simpkins did a set rate for each photo and that was that. But Nat couldn't let her get away. Her picture would be such a draw.

"Very well. Where would you like me to stand?"

Well, it was too late to back out now. She had accepted his offer. He'd think of something to tell Mr Simpkins later.

"'Um . . .'" Nat looked round in what he hoped was a professional manner. And then he saw it — the perfect setting. "How about by the boat?"

The sea breeze ruffled the hem of her skirt as she perched on the upturned tub, which was used to advertise trips round the bay.

"Shall I hold the oar?"

"Good idea." Nat snapped away. He was only supposed to take one shot but, sensing something was going on, a little group of onlookers had gathered around and success was going to Nat's head. He told himself that Mr Simpkins would be pleased with all the extra publicity.

"You a professional?" an awed schoolboy asked.

"I am indeed. Now, I must ask for quiet."

"Cor!" His young fan was clearly impressed and lapsed into silence.

Ten minutes later, Nat couldn't think of any more reasons to detain his subject and regretfully he replaced his lens cover. Thank goodness he'd remembered to take it off — and to keep his fingers away from the viewfinder.

Sensing the entertainment was over, the crowd began to drift off.

"What now?" the vision of loveliness asked.

"What we do," Nat explained with what he hoped was a note of authority in his voice, "is we develop the film overnight then display the photos on our board the next day."

"I've seen some of your shots. They look very professional."

Nat had the grace to blush. He very much doubted she had seen any of *his* work.

"May I have your name, please?" he asked, getting out his notebook.

"Elsie Hammond."

"Thank you, Miss Hammond." He added her name to his list then raised his boater again. "I hope to see you tomorrow."

NAT stared at Mr Simpkins in horror. It couldn't be true.

"No film?"

"Look for yourself."

Mr Simpkins thrust his camera at him. The back was open. A black hole stared back at him where the film was supposed to be. It was true. Nat had forgotten to load the camera.

"I d-don't k-know what happened," he stuttered.

"I do." Mr Simpkins's face was red with annoyance. "You're incompetent. You can man the hut today and explain to the disappointed holidaymakers why we've no new photos to display."

Nat couldn't blame Mr Simpkins for being cross. It was the height of the season and he'd lost them a whole day's work. How could he have been so stupid?

When he'd been offered this job at short notice, he'd leaped at the chance. He loved talking to people and a job in the open air was so much better than sitting in a stuffy office adding up boring columns of figures.

He would never be offered a permanent job now.

He watched Mr Simpkins stomp off down the esplanade then opened up the hut and sat down on the little stool. The few remaining unclaimed snapshots hardly filled the board. Nat wished he had something to cover the gaps.

He felt something stiff in his back pocket as he wriggled uncomfortably on his stool. His first day's snapshots — he had forgotten about them.

He looked at the boots and the family whose heads he'd managed to cut off. A reluctant smile curved his lips as a germ of an idea came to him.

＊　　＊　　＊　　＊

"What's going on?" Mr Simpkins demanded as he returned to the hut, hot and tired after his day's work.

The crowd was three deep round the photo display. Everyone was laughing and Nat appeared to be doing a roaring trade.

"Fine lad you've got there, Simpkins," the owner of the boat trip company informed him. "Got us all guessing where the photo was taken. As for the headless family, haven't laughed so much in years. Good idea of yours." He patted Mr Simpkins on the back. "Must be on my way. All this extra activity has been wonderful for business, I'll tell you that."

Mr Simpkins struggled to the front of the crowd to where Nat was busy taking money and scribbling notes on bits of paper.

"Nat?" He looked round in disbelief.

"Oh, hello, Mr Simpkins. Right, that's it," he announced to the crowd. "Results will appear tomorrow."

"What are you talking about?" Mr Simpkins demanded as the last customers left, clutching their slips of paper.

"I, er, ran a competition. I hope you don't mind, and — well, look."

NAT waved a hand at the noticeboard. In the middle was the pair of boots. A free photo was the prize offered to anyone who could correctly identify the location of the photograph.

Next to it was the headless family under which Nat had written *One I Got Wrong But I'm Learning!*

"And I promised all the disappointed customers I'd take another photo of them tomorrow."

Mr Simpkins scratched his head. He wasn't at all sure what was going on, but young Nat seemed to have packed in the crowds. He was a likeable lad and no mistake and he certainly had a way with the customers.

"If there is a tomorrow," he said. It wouldn't do to let the lad get above himself, especially as he'd made up his mind to keep him on. He had initiative and Mr Simpkins liked that, but there was no harm in keeping him on tenterhooks a bit longer.

He looked at the board again.

"Who is Elsie Hammond?" he asked.

Nat flushed a deep red. Elsie had been his one disappointment of the day. She hadn't arrived for her photos and, as it was now nearly six o'clock, Nat doubted she would turn up.

"And why is she doing the prize draw tomorrow?" Mr Simpkins went on.

"She's the young lady I was telling you about," Nat mumbled. "The one whose pictures I took . . ."

"Didn't take," Mr Simpkins reminded him.

"They were good pictures." Nat looked so earnest, Mr Simpkins felt sorry for him. "Only she didn't turn up today, so I thought . . ."

"Putting her name on the noticeboard would get her here tomorrow?"

"Something like that," Nat admitted. "I'm sorry. I suppose it's not good business practice?"

"We'll talk about it in the morning."

"If you're going to fire me, I'd rather know about it now. Please," Nat added. How he would hate sitting in a stuffy office all day, watching the sun through the window and longing to be outside in the fresh air.

"I'm sure you would, young man." Mr Simpkins tried to frown at him, but it didn't really work. "But tomorrow will do. Besides, there's a young lady in a gingham dress running down the esplanade, and, unless I'm very much mistaken, she's your Elsie."

IN an instant, Nat swung round.

"Nat." She laughed and somehow landed up in his arms. "What's going on? Why on earth did you put my name up like that?"

Nat blinked.

"I wanted to see you again," he admitted. "And when you didn't turn up for your photos . . ."

"How do you do, Miss —?" Mr Simpkins interrupted.

"Hammond." Elsie smiled. "I work in Maureen's Modes and we had such a busy day I couldn't get away.

"All the customers were talking about your display. Then someone wanted to know when I was doing the prize draw. What's it all about?"

Nat looked at Mr Simpkins, who took the hint.

"Off you go, lad," he said, nodding to the pair of them. "I'll close up. See you in the morning, Nat. Nine o'clock sharp." He raised his hat to Elsie then began looking round for his keys.

"Are you free this evening?" Nat asked her tentatively.

"I could be." She smiled.

"Why don't we go and have a cup of tea and I can show you how to take photographs?"

*　　*　　*　　*

People were beginning to arrive. Nat's assistant was standing by the door, welcoming them and handing out brochures.

Nat caught the scent of bluebells. He turned round.

"You're old-fashioned, did you know that?" He watched Elsie inspect her picture. "According to my assistant, that is."

Her lips curved into a smile.

"We got a free boat trip round the bay from the proprietor for all the extra publicity we created. Do you remember?"

Nat grinned.

"I don't know how I plucked up the courage to propose to you on that trip. I'd only known you two days."

"I'm glad you did." Elsie slipped her hand into his. "Shall we go and greet our guests?"

It had been a lucky day when he'd met Elsie, Nat thought, as they made their way to the door. He knew she was the girl for him and his instinct had never let him down. ■

W E need some more sea for the moat!"

Daniella danced excitedly beside the sandcastle that rose in a mound of turrets out of the golden beach.

Emily, wielding the spade and quite impressed with her sandcastle-building skills — but then she had built one yesterday, and the day before — passed her the bright red bucket that they'd bought from a kiosk on the promenade above the sea wall.

"You fetch some, then, darling." She watched as her little daughter ran a few yards over the sand to where the little waves sighed in on to the beach.

It wasn't particularly warm on the east coast for the first week in August. Sea and sky were grey where she'd prefer to see blue, and the wind tossed her hair with wild fingers. But the beach was busy with laughing families and none of the children seemed to mind being bundled into cardigans as they played.

Emily listened to the wistful cries of the gulls and the squeaky-crunchy sound of sand being dug all around her; the laughter from a boy as his father

Illustration by Tony Paul, from his book "How To Paint From Photographs", New Holland Publishers.

tried to direct a frisbee and the wind kept throwing it back. She smiled at the boy's joy and wished that Martin was here to play with Daniella like that.

But Martin couldn't get away. He was just so busy at work — as usual — and so Emily had come to stay with her brother and his wife near Hunstanton so that at least she and Daniella could have a holiday.

HE sighed. A last-minute brainwave on her part, it hadn't been such a good idea as she'd first thought. Robbie had been enthusiastic at first. "Of course you can come! It'll be lovely to see you." Then he'd hesitated before qualifying his invitation.

"Our diaries are full to bursting, as usual, but you and Daniella will only want to use our place as a base, won't you?

"Yes — come for as long as you like!"

Robbie and Carole, not having children to consider, revelled in extremely busy lives. Each worked full time and spent their leisure hours racing from badminton to squash to dance classes. That was when they weren't doing

All Work And No Play...

by Sue Moorcroft.

their Scuba training. They did everything together — including the dancing — and it was all depressingly cosy, especially when Emily couldn't persuade Martin to take even one week off from the business for a family break.

The business, the business . . . Their entire lives revolved around the business. The Biz, they called it. Martin had left the company he had been working for and begun the Biz over a year ago, and from that first moment it had become the tyrant that ruled their lives.

Martin worked long hours building up the tool hire business, smartening up the rented premises, making leaflets on the computer to put through letter-boxes to tempt customers into hiring his equipment for their DIY, doing the books, seeing the accountant . . . Open for the main weekend trade and most of the week as well, the Biz saw a lot more of him than Emily and Daniella ever did.

"Summer's not the time to take a week off," he'd claimed, looking frazzled, as usual. "Everyone's hiring Rotavators to churn up their lawns so that they can put trendy decking down."

Emily had felt a familiar prickle of annoyance.

"And the autumn won't be any better because then customers are sanding and staining their floors ready to impress the Christmas relatives. After Christmas it'll be slack and you'll be worried to death that you miss a single one of the few customers there are — then in the spring they'll begin again with their gardens.

"Exactly when *is* the time for a holiday?"

"I've got to earn money to feed us all, Emily," Martin had replied quietly. But she could tell he was injured by her exasperation.

And she understood how important the Biz was. But, oh, she wished she and Daniella came ahead of it on the list of priorities just occasionally!

Martin loved them both, she knew he did, and he was a great dad — when he could grab the time. But the Biz only let him come home just in time for a few minutes' play and a story curled together on Daniella's bed. Days when he could play with her for hours on a beach seemed to be at an end.

✳   ✳   ✳   ✳

Daniella was already chattering away in the adorably jumbled way that went with being barely three. How could Martin stand to be away from her so much?

Daniella turned now and beamed at Emily, pointing to her bucket.

"I got walker!"

"Water," Emily corrected gently. "Shall we pour it into the moat?"

But Daniella's attention was already on another little girl, a little older than herself, who was patrolling the high-water line and filling her bucket with glistening shells.

"I'm Harriet," the little girl announced after inspecting Daniella solemnly.

Daniella's face lit up.

"'Lo, Harriet. I'm Daniella!"

"We can be friends!" Harriet edged closer.

"I like friends," Daniella confided and, tipping the water from her bucket, she promptly joined Harriet in gathering shells.

From one sandcastle over, a laughing voice called to Emily.

"Oh, bless them! They make life worthwhile, don't they?"

Quite pleased at the prospect of a little adult conversation, Emily grinned.

"I don't know what else does, if they don't!"

Harriet's mother was a little older and her hair was plaited into a rope down her back. With her cut-off jeans and well-worn trainers, she looked perfectly at home on the beach. She waved a fat red flask at Emily.

"Cuppa? I can spare some."

"That would be brilliant!"

And in no time they'd moved their beach towels together.

Harriet's mother introduced herself as Fiona and they drank tea and watched the two little blonde girls giggling at the coldness on their toes as they skipped about in the lacy fringes of the sea.

Then Fiona had the idea of digging waterways between their two sandcastles and joining them up with the sea. And so the afternoon passed in laughter and fun.

THEY met again the following day. It was great having someone to chat with; Fiona was good company, interested in others and a good listener. It wasn't long before Emily found herself indulging in a little grumble about Martin not being able to join them at the coast because of the Biz.

Fiona shielded her eyes from the sun and shrugged.

"But he's working so hard because of you and Daniella."

Emily didn't think it was quite as straightforward as that.

"Well . . . he began the business because he didn't get on with his old boss. But when he was working for somebody he didn't work even half the hours he does now, and his salary was secure."

Fiona flicked her plait back over one shoulder.

"I think a man who works hard and provides for his family should be appreciated, to be honest. It's all very well you having the odd week or two on your own with Daniella when you're on holiday and probably have enough money for treats. But I can assure you that it's different if you're alone for the long haul, a single parent day in and day out. Especially if the financial responsibility has turned out to be all yours, too!"

There was silence. Emily didn't like to fish for information, but she sensed Fiona spoke from experience and tried to change the subject.

"Shall we meet up tomorrow? I've promised Daniella a ride on the little train up to the headland."

Fiona smiled wistfully.

"I only wish we could — but Harriet and I could only afford a long weekend. We have to catch the coach home tomorrow."

The weather continued to be cool and windy and Emily and Daniella missed Fiona and Harriet. Robbie and Carole went on racketing about their busy lives with scarcely time to sit down for a family meal, and Emily and Daniella roamed about the beach and the town.

"Daddy's van?" Daniella looked up at Emily, her face one big question mark as she pointed at a passing white van.

"I'm afraid not, darling. It's just a van like Daddy's; there are lots of them about."

Daniella's disappointment was obvious and Emily gave her a big cuddle. She

The End Of Summer

*THE scent of mown hay on a late
    summer's day,
The heavy air heady as wine,
The poppies all blowsy, the bees feeling
    drowsy,
As on nature's nectar they dine.*

*We feel languid and lazy when mornings
    are hazy
And the mist slowly melts in the sun;
The gardens have peaked (and our poor
    backs have creaked!)
But we're proud of the work that we've
    done.*

*Fallen petals and nettles and weeds on
    the paths —
All the things that we're too tired to clear,
Soon we'll feel autumn's chill and of
    course then we will
Decide what we'll tackle next year!*

— Eileen Hay.

knew exactly how her daughter felt — because Emily was missing Martin, too!

With only Daniella for company on the beach, Emily had plenty of time to reflect on what Fiona had said, and her conscience began to jab at her. Martin was much happier working for himself than for his old boss. It was evident in the way he dashed off to work every morning with a grin and a wink. And he insisted — although she'd found it a bit difficult to believe, sometimes — that it wouldn't be for ever that the Biz took up so much of his time.

"Things should be easier after the first two years," he'd promised. "When the start-up loan is repaid I'll be able to employ somebody to work with me and a lot of the pressure will be off."

It was true that he didn't see as much of Daniella as he'd like . . . but he saw as much of her as he could.

Collecting shells and making patterns out of pebbles, Emily's mind worked and worked, putting Fiona's quiet words to her conscience and reason.

Without saying it directly, she knew Fiona had thought that Emily had been looking at things a bit one-sidedly.

✳   ✳   ✳   ✳

At the sound of a key in the lock, Daniella flew to her feet and bounded to the door.

"Daddy!"

R. Gauld

Rushing in, Martin nearly fell over her. His eyes grew big with amazement.

"Hello, you two! What a brilliant surprise! What are you doing home? Is everything OK?" He swung Daniella up into his arms for a big hug, pressing his cheek against hers and cradling her little frame in his arms.

Emily hovered awkwardly behind Daniella in the hall.

"There's nothing wrong. We just decided we'd rather be at home."

"Daddy, we having a lovely picnic!"

"Picnic?" Eyebrows raised, Martin looked at Daniella and then at the soft summer rain trickling down the hall window.

"Quick! I'll show you!" Daniella wriggled to be set down, grabbing Martin's hand and hauling him down the hall and into the sitting-room.

EMILY followed uncertainly, blushing in case Martin thought what she'd done was silly. She found him inspecting the blue-chequered cloth spread on the floor and set with cheerful plastic cups and plates. A cool-box full of food she'd prepared during the afternoon stood beside a neatly folded stack of paper napkins.

"I hungry," Daniella announced, sitting cross-legged on the carpet at one corner of the cloth.

Emily giggled as she copied her.

"Would you care to join us?"

"I'd be delighted!" Martin folded his long frame down on the carpet as Emily took chicken pieces, salad and soft rolls from the cool-box.

"Cress!" Daniella squeaked happily. "Mummy, cress is my favourite!"

While she was occupied eating her cress, one stalk at a time, Martin leaned over and kissed Emily softly.

"This is fantastic. I can't believe you're here. Why did you decide to come home?"

"We missed you so very much." She returned his kiss. "And I suddenly

91

realised what should have been obvious — for all my complaints that you don't see enough of Daniella, my taking her away for a fortnight ensured you saw her even less!

"And . . . and I wanted to tell you that I realise you deserve to be happy in your work, and if it's the Biz that makes you happy, then we'll have to work around it for a bit.

"Now Daniella's at playgroup, I could even do some of the book-work for you. For us," she corrected.

S O, I thought the best thing would be if we have our holiday in little bits when you get home in the evenings. We'll keep Daniella up a bit later and have picnics and barbecues." She shot a scathing look outside. "In the garden, if the weather ever clears up!"

Martin laughed, eyes dancing.

"I like some bread," Daniella announced.

Emily paused, disconcerted by Martin's laughter, as she placed a soft buttered roll on to Daniella's plate.

"I know it's not much of a holiday, but I thought it might be better than being at opposite ends of the country!"

With a huge grin, Martin threw his arms around her.

"I've realised this past week that anything's better than that! The Biz is important, but it's not as important as you two. Nothing is. And if I can't find a way to have even a break with you, the Biz isn't worth having.

"So I asked Dad to hold the fort for a few days — he leapt at the chance, now he's retired. And I rushed home tonight intending to throw a few things in a holdall and drive up in the van to surprise you!"

"Chicken, please," Daniella demanded, cress stuck all over her damp fingers.

Emily passed her both chicken and a napkin without taking her eyes from Martin.

"Really? So you've got a few days off, and we can do things together?" She could scarcely believe her ears. "Hooray!"

"Hooray!" Daniella agreed, flinging her arms out and accidentally poking her daddy in the face with her piece of chicken.

Laughing as he wiped his face, Martin pulled Emily and Daniella closer to him.

"Everything that's most important to me in the world is sitting right here on this picnic-blanket. And we're going to enjoy each other's company, and remember that." ■

Cadgwith, Cornwall, England

*W*HEN our children were small we often holidayed in scenic Cadgwith, in Cornwall. Only a few hours' drive from home, with wonderful weather and lots to do, it really was our idea of the perfect holiday spot.

Our favourite place was the Little Cove, a sandy beach with boulders, and we could spend all day there, swimming and playing. I used to pack a huge picnic and we would stay for lunch and tea as the children often lost track of time. A local wet fish shop had the most marvellous seafood for sale and a host of recipe ideas for you to try. I still use one for monkfish to this day, and it's become a real family favourite over the years.

I have very fond memories of our holidays in Cadgwith and am pleased to say that my son has been back there with his own children recently. He had a marvellous time and it looks like a new generation of our family is going to enjoy this lovely spot all over again.

I just wanted to say thank you, my "Friend", for bringing back all those wonderful memories. Your cover artwork was better than a tonic!

— **Mrs Y.H., London.**

J. CAMPBELL KERR.

See You Later

by Kate Blackadder.

"NO tickets left?" Lizzie looked at the girl in the Book Festival box office in dismay. "But I promised my nephew I'd take him. J.K. Rowling's his favourite author."

The girl looked sympathetic.

"I'm sorry, she's been sold out for weeks. Perhaps you'd like to have a look at our programme? There are lots of other events for children."

"Thank you."

Lizzie took a programme and moved through into Charlotte Square gardens, transformed as always for two weeks each August by tents of all shapes and sizes.

Typical, she thought. Every year she meant to get organised for all the festivals there were in summer in Edinburgh. Maybe that was the problem — there was just so much going on! By the time she decided what she wanted to see, it was always too late.

Tommy would be disappointed, but maybe there was someone else he would like.

At the back of the big book tent was a café selling cakes and coffee. Lizzie looked at her watch. There was just time for a *latte*, and maybe one of those scrumptious-looking brownies, before she had to get back to her work in the design department of the museum. She paid for the coffee, put a lid on it, and took her tray outside so she could sit at one of the little tables with an umbrella in the middle while she read the programme.

If Tommy had been younger they could have gone to a Bob the Builder event, or sat cross-legged in a tepee and listened to fairy tales. But at twelve he was harder to please.

As Lizzie flicked through the rest of the programme the name *Angus Fraser*

Alligator

Illustration by William Webb.

jumped out at her. She could recall Tommy telling her about a documentary he'd seen on television, about an explorer who had to wrestle with an alligator on his last expedition to a remote area of South America. Wasn't that his name? Angus Fraser. She stared at his photograph excitedly while she bit into the brownie. Angus Fraser was going to be *here*, at the Edinburgh Book Festival, *this* Saturday. Tomorrow!

"EXCUSE me. Is this seat free?"

Lizzie looked up. Reddish hair, was her first thought. Red-gold really. Bit older than her, about thirty perhaps. Soft Scottish island accent. Broad shoulders.

"Yes, yes it is."

The man put his coffee and a newspaper down on the table, and nodded

95

towards Lizzie's brownie.

"Maybe I should have got one of those. I haven't had any lunch. Do you recommend them?"

"Mmm." Lizzie gulped and swallowed. "Delicious. But the flapjacks looked good, too. More healthy, more of a lunch thing?"

He laughed.

"Maybe you're right. Would you mind keeping this seat while I go and debate the issue?"

Lizzie nodded.

"Tricky decision," she said. "Good luck."

WHEN he reappeared, his paper plate bore a brownie and a flapjack. He broke the flapjack and put half on Lizzie's plate.

"Try a bit of this."

They chewed in companionable silence for a bit.

When the last crumb had been eaten he sighed.

"The pecan tarts looked good, too. I'll maybe try one tomorrow. What do you think?"

"And those little custard things? Good idea. Work your way round them all."

Lizzie wiped her fingers on a paper napkin and tore the top off her coffee carton.

He put his own coffee down and leaned across the table.

"Do you mind if I tell you something? You don't have to take the lid off. Lift up this bit here. See?"

Lizzie burst out laughing.

"I've drunk tons of these, and I never knew that. No more spills, or burnt fingers. You've changed my life. Thank you!"

The man with the red-gold hair smiled. It was a lovely smile, Lizzie thought, making his blue-green eyes shine like the sea on a summer's day.

"It's my pleasure, Lizzie."

"How do you . . .?" she began and laughed again as she realised that he was looking at her name on her museum pass.

"I'm Angus. Are you going to any of the events here today?"

"No, I'm just here to get . . ." She stopped and peered across the table, and then down at the photograph in the programme and back to him. Angus? Angus, the alligator man!

"I'm just here to get tickets for my nephew. And me. Yes, tickets for my nephew and me, for Saturday. I hope there are some left," she babbled.

"Gosh, it must seem very cold to you here, after all those hot places. Swamps and things."

"Swamps . . .?" He raised his eyebrows, but Lizzie rushed on.

"And jungles. And those alligators! It must have been terrifying."

"It must have been," Angus agreed, looking at her curiously.

Calm down, Lizzie told herself, you're behaving like a complete idiot. She took a deep breath, the way she remembered being taught in the yoga class she'd gone to before she'd switched to making jewellery, and drank her coffee too quickly.

"Nice to meet you, er, Angus." She coughed. "Sorry, I must dash — got to get tickets for, well, for myself and . . ."

"Your nephew," Angus finished.

"Tommy, my nephew. A great fan of yours." She waved her hands around wildly, catching sight of her watch. "Is that the time? I must get back to work."

"Lizzie!" Angus put out a hand to stop her tripping over a guy rope. "What's your second name? I'd like . . ."

"Lyall. Lizzie Lyall," she called over her shoulder.

"I'm Angus."

"Oh, I know who you are," Lizzie said, disappearing. "You're Angus. The Alligator Man."

S O, Tommy," she said over supper at her sister's that night. She took the Book Festival programme from her bag. "Tomorrow, how would you like to see — tra la tra la! — Angus Fraser! I got tickets today; there weren't many left.

"And I actually met him, and he was really nice. Gorgeous, actually. Bluey-green eyes for seeing across alligator-infested rivers."

"Who?"

"Angus Fraser, the explorer you were telling me about. The Alligator Man."

"Alex *Farrar* is the Alligator Man, Auntie Lizzie. What are you talking about?"

"Oh, no!" Lizzie grabbed the programme and read the page — properly, this time.

"I thought . . ." She felt herself grow hot. "Oh, no. *Skye hotelier Angus Fraser will be reading from his debut novel, 'Tourist Trap', a darkly funny tale of mystery and murder in a Highland village . . .*"

She looked at his photograph again. He may never have wrestled with an alligator, but he was still gorgeous, even in black and white.

"Cool," Tommy said excitedly. "Sounds just like Harry Potter."

But his mother interrupted, raising her eyebrows at her sister before turning to her excited son.

"I'm afraid not, Tommy. I don't think Angus Fraser sounds right for you. I think his novel is just a bit too grown up."

"Tommy, I'm sorry," Lizzie apologised. "I'll take you to the movies and for a pizza on Sunday afternoon instead. OK?"

"Cool," Tommy said again.

THERE was a magical air about the gardens today, Lizzie thought, as she rushed past the queue of excited J.K. Rowling fans on Saturday. Maybe it was the buzz of anticipation, or maybe the sun, dappling leaf patterns on to the white tents.

She'd spent a sleepless night, wondering whether or not to go to hear Angus speaking. After all, he must have thought she was a mad woman, Angus who *wasn't* the Alligator Man. She had decided eventually to get there early, and sit at the back.

But in the morning she had an idea for a new brooch, and by the time she had sketched it out and threaded the little golden beads together she had just twenty minutes to run to Charlotte Square.

The event was just about to start. The attendant hurried her in to sit down in a seat in the middle of the third row. Eight people had to stand up to let her past, and she tripped over someone's handbag. The man with the red-gold hair on the stage looked out into the audience to see what the commotion was about.

"Lizzie!" Angus Fraser jumped up, forgetting about the microphone which had just been attached to his lapel. It fell off.

"Lizzie!" he shouted. "Hello! I'm sorry I'm not Angus the Alligator Man, but will you wait for me afterwards? Please?"

Lizzie smiled and waved and settled into her seat, feeling a blush engulf her face. A ripple of laughter went through the audience and everyone craned their necks to stare at her. She was thankful when their attention turned back to the stage.

It would be difficult to have an explorer for a boyfriend, Lizzie reflected. He would be away a lot, obviously. Or he might want her to wrestle with alligators, too, and stumble through dangerous swamps after him — miles away from hot baths and chocolate brownies and book festivals.

A novelist who ran a hotel, on the other hand . . .

She looked down at her new brooch. From among the golden beads a glittering, ruby-coloured eye winked back at her. Come to think of it, though, she'd always have a soft spot for alligators. ■

Pig In The Middle

by Pamela Kavanagh.

Illustration by David Young.

CHERYL kicked mutinously at a stone on the path, sending it spinning and creating a small dust-storm that blew up in her face and settled grubbily on her pale pink T-shirt.

Oh, no! Now she'd get told off for getting dirty and she was already in enough trouble as it was. Not that it had been her fault.

Cheryl sighed. The blame really lay with her brother. Well, foster brother, actually. If Zack hadn't dared her to go into the pig pasture after the football, she wouldn't have opened the gate and the pigs wouldn't have got out and trashed Mum's vegetable plot.

"Cheryl! What am I to do with you?" Mum, standing there red-faced and furious amongst the shattered pea canes and trampled salad greens, had gone ballistic. "How often do you need to be told always to close the gates?"

"I was doing it," Cheryl tried to explain. "They just pushed their way in."

It was true. The pigs had been rooting happily in the hedgerow on the far side of the pasture. How was she to know that Miranda's beady little eyes were on her? Dad had told her that pigs were the canniest creatures on the farm, and Miranda, the prize Black Spot, had to be the canniest of the lot.

"There goes Miranda," he would say. "Always up to something!"

Bit like me, Cheryl thought, sending another stone skittering across the path. Saturday was her birthday. With luck the adoption news would be through by then. Just lately, though, she had got into one scrape after another. Would the couple she had come to call Mum and Dad still want her? Cheryl sighed.

"Hey, Cheryl!"

Cheryl turned to see Zack loping towards her along the path, sunlight turning his mop of hair to fire. Cheryl's hair was a lighter, reddish-blonde colour. To see them together, anyone would think that they really were brother and sister.

H I," Cheryl said. "Where did you skive off to?"

"I didn't. I went to fetch the football and when I got back you'd cleared off. Mum sent me to find you."

"Is she still going on about what happened?"

"A bit. I'm sorry. I didn't mean to get you in trouble."

"It's OK." Cheryl gave him a small smile. With his freckled face and merry blue eyes, it was impossible to be mad at Zack for long.

They fell into step, heading back to the farm that Mum and Dad had taken over when Gran and Grandpa retired. Cheryl had been seven then and newly fostered. She could still remember the thrill of having her very own bedroom with the view across the fields.

"Did Mum say anything about cancelling my birthday party?"

"Of course not." Zack looked at her like she was mad. "Why should she?"

"Thought she might, that's all. I'd hate for it to be called off."

Cheryl was really looking forward to her birthday party this year. She had invited lots of her schoolfriends and didn't want to have to let them down if the party was cancelled.

"Zack . . ." Cheryl swallowed, then started again. "You don't think they'll change their minds about me, do you?"

"What? About the adoption, you mean? Course not, stupid! The garden was a mess, though. We could tidy it up a bit, I suppose. Mum'd like that."

"Good idea." Heartened, Cheryl gave a little skip. "Only five days to go and I'll be ten. What's it like being ten, Zack?"

"Not bad. Eleven's better. Eleven's cool. Come on. Race you back!"

They went sprinting down the hillside, Cheryl's ponytail bouncing. On reaching the farm and the havoc that only that morning had been neat rows of soft fruit and vegetables, the sound of raised voices coming from the barn pulled them up short.

CHILDREN will be children and pigs will be pigs!" Dad's measured tones carried on the warm air. "I'm sorry about what's happened, Olwyn. But it's not the end of the world."

"It's the end of my peas and lettuce! And they were doing so well."

"Aye well, you'd have been better keeping the garden on the far side of the house where it always used to be, right away from any stock. It's plain common sense."

"Don't talk to me about sense," Olwyn said sharply. "Where's the sense in growing stuff that'd be in the shade half the day? I'm serious, Gregory. What's needed here is a decent stock fence and properly sprung gates. Then the animals might stay put!"

"You're right there! Thing is, there are only so many hours in the day. For now all I can do is patch up the gaps in the hedges. A better job will have to wait till winter when I've got more time."

The children listened in horror. Their parents never quarrelled. What was going on?

"Oh, no," Cheryl said woefully. "This is all my fault."

"Wasn't. It was mine. I shouldn't have kicked the ball there in the first place. Let's try to sort out the garden for Mum, maybe that will make her feel better."

They were heading for the tool shed when Mum called them in for lunch. Her eyes went straight to Cheryl's grubby T-shirt.

"Cheryl, what have you been doing? Rolling in the dirt? Go and change that top. And wash your hands, both of you."

Thinking over what had happened that day already, the two children obeyed without a murmur.

✳   ✳   ✳   ✳

As if the day had not been traumatic enough, that evening something happened to top it all. Gregory Massey was doing the final rounds of the stock and, casting an eye over the free-ranging pigs in their pasture, he saw that Miranda was not amongst them.

"I don't know where she can be," he said, coming in and sighing. "I've had a look around but there's no sign. I can't do any more tonight. It's too dark."

"How did she get out?"

"Pushed through a weak spot in the hedge, I suppose. Had a taste of freedom, didn't she? Stands to reason she'd want more."

"She can't have gone far. I'll help you look for her tomorrow." Olwyn bit her lip. "I'm sorry I was snippy with you this morning, Gregory. I didn't mean it."

"I know."

"It's this waiting, it's driving me mad! Surely we should have heard from the adoption people by now? I'm certain it didn't take this long with Zack."

"I think it did, you know. I remember we were both on pins at the time. Try not to worry too much. Cheryl's been with us for nearly three years. We've an excellent record for fostering. There's no reason for it not to go through."

"I know, but I love her to bits, Gregory. If she were taken from us, I don't think I could bear it! And then I went and shouted at her today. I felt awful afterwards. All over a silly garden, too."

Beyond the window, an owl called throatily to its mate as they went to bed. It seemed like an omen to Olwyn. She crossed her fingers that, maybe tomorrow, that all-important letter would be in the post.

FOR Cheryl, Miranda's untimely disappearance did nothing to improve her feeling of trepidation. Next day at breakfast, she listened in silence to her father's account of the fruitless early morning search.

"We've looked all over the place! She's nowhere to be found."

"Will Miranda come back by herself?" Zack asked.

"Probably. Once she gets tired of her own company," Mum said from the stove where she was making more toast. She brought the plate to the table. "Better hurry, Zack. Your lift will be here shortly."

Cheryl's heart sank even further. She had forgotten that Zack was going to visit his best mate and would be away all day — neatly putting paid to their plan to sort out the garden.

"I'd best be making tracks myself." Gregory Massey stood up abruptly. "The contractors are due at eight."

"But you haven't touched your toast," Olwyn said.

"No time. Let's hope we get the silage in before the weather breaks. See you later. Cheers, you two. Be good."

Ruffling the children's hair affectionately, he left the kitchen. Soon afterwards Zack's lift arrived and off he went. Left alone with her mother, Cheryl looked about to see how she could be helpful. She reached for the discarded toast.

"Shall I put this in the pig bin, Mum?"

"No, it's all right, thanks. I'll have it myself. Mind you keep away from the fields today, Cheryl. Dad's busy. They won't want you getting underfoot."

"OK." Cheryl bit her lip, and then said, "Mum, is it my fault that Miranda's left home?"

"She hasn't left home." Olwyn's lips twitched. "What a funny girl you are. And of course it isn't your fault. Pigs are very inquisitive, and this is Miranda, remember. Of all of them, she's the one most likely to lead us a dance."

"Bit like me, you mean."

"You could say that!" The quirk became a full-blown grin. "Don't worry.

Step Back In Time

Abraham Lincoln

THE sixteenth president of the United States of America was born on his parents' farm in Hardin County, Kentucky, on February 12, 1809.

Lincoln was most famous for implementing measures to abolish slavery by issuing the Emancipation Proclamation in 1863 and encouraging the passing of the Thirteenth Amendment in 1865.

Lincoln was also famous for his beard.

On October 15, 1860, a few weeks before he was elected president, Lincoln received a letter from eleven-year-old Grace Bedell who had written to encourage him to grow a beard.

All the ladies like whiskers, she wrote, *and they would tease their husbands to vote for you and then you would be president.*

Lincoln replied on October 19, asking whether Grace thought that growing a beard would be a "silly affectation" as he had never had one before.

However, within a month, he grew his now-famous beard and went on to become president of the USA.

He later met Grace, and a statue in Westfield, New York commemorates this encounter.

Abraham Lincoln served as president for four years before he was assassinated by John Wilkes Booth in Ford's Theatre, Washington DC.

Booth went on the run, but was cornered in a tobacco barn and was shot himself by a Union Army soldier. ■

Most likely she'll be back before the day's out. If you should see her, give me a shout and we'll put her back in with the others together. OK?"

"OK."

OLWYN began buttering her rapidly cooling toast and Cheryl wandered outside. With Zack not here, Mum somehow not quite herself and Dad occupied with the silaging, the day stretched endlessly ahead. Coming to the once green and lush vegetable plot, Cheryl pulled to a stop. Under the bright glare of the morning sun, the damaged plants looked worse than ever.

A thought struck. Why not get on with the work herself? Cheryl looked down at her T-shirt — pale blue today — and decided that she wasn't going to make the same mistake twice. She'd better change it for something more suitable.

From the utility room she could hear the hum of the washing machine and her mother singing quietly to herself as she sorted the laundry. Running upstairs to her bedroom, Cheryl rummaged through the chest of drawers for a sludgy coloured shirt she knew she had somewhere.

Not finding it, and not stopping to tidy up behind her, Cheryl slipped into her mother's room and borrowed a top instead — a slinky black one she thought wouldn't show the dirt. Then, swapping her shorts for workmanlike jeans, she went back outside and ran down to the garden.

Starting on the row of peas, Cheryl pulled out the broken stems and chucked them aside. Some of the plants looked all right, but she yanked them out anyway to make a neater job of it. Every so often she would pause to pop a pea pod and eat the sweet little morsels inside, her mind still grappling with the uneasy situation at home.

Having enough of the peas, Cheryl moved on to the strawberry bed. It grew hot as she worked and now and again she stopped to wipe her sweaty and dirty hands down the front of her top.

From the far side of the house she could hear Mum calling for her.

"Cheryl, where are you? There's juice and biscuits on the kitchen table. I'm taking Dad and the workforce their elevenses. I won't be long."

Giving up for the moment, Cheryl trotted off in search of that much needed refreshment.

THERE you go." Raising her voice above the roar of machinery, Olwyn handed her husband the hamper of food. "There's canned drinks and coffee in the flasks for those who prefer it. And you've got biscuits and fruit cake."

"Just the job. Thanks!"

"No problem. How's it going?"

"Not bad at all. At least the weather's held. Come over by the trees for a moment out of this din . . . That's better. Has the post been yet?"

"Yes, but nothing of any importance," Olwyn told him with a sigh.

"Bear up. It'll come."

"Yes, but will it be the news we want? The longer it goes on, the more doubtful I get. I couldn't sleep last night for thinking about it."

"I think it's getting to all of us, not least Cheryl. Zack said something about her being concerned that we don't want her."

"Really?" Olwyn was horrified. "Why on earth should she think that?"

"Oh, something to do with that incident with the pigs and the veg plot. You know children. They get these notions."

"All the same, we must reassure her. I've purposely not said too much for fear of worrying Cheryl. Seems you can never get it right!"

"True. If we don't hear something by the end of the week it might be as well to do some chasing up. Meantime, we keep smiling and hope this weather lasts for Saturday's birthday bash. Any sign of Miranda yet?"

"Not as such. I think Cheryl has stationed herself on lookout. If Miranda turns up, I'm sure we'll know about it."

The tractors had ground to a halt and the drivers were now heading for the gate and the food hamper. Gregory took his leave of his wife and Olwyn headed back to the farmhouse. Instead of going indoors, however, she went to cast a calmer eye over the garden. There, she came to an abrupt stop.

What on earth had been going on? Some of the pea plants that had survived the onslaught now lay in yellowing piles all over the ground. Some of the strawberries were the same. There could only be one answer.

CHERYL?"

Hastening to the house, she found the little girl sitting on the kitchen step with a handful of chocolate biscuits.

"Cheryl, what's been going on with my garden? And what are you doing wearing my best silk top! Look at the state of it!"

Cheryl looked down at the black silk that hung loosely on her slight frame and was looking absolutely awful.

"I only borrowed it. I couldn't find my khaki shirt and I didn't want to mess up my other things."

"So you messed up my expensive top instead? Oh, Cheryl, what were you thinking of?"

"Nothing!" Cheryl jumped to her feet, her lip trembling. "I only wanted to help! I wanted to clear up the garden after the pigs had trashed it. I wanted to surprise you and now it's all spoilt! And I bet you and Dad won't want me any more!"

Sinking down on to the step beside the woebegone figure, Olwyn took her in her arms and rocked her gently.

"Darling Cheryl, Dad and I will always want you. You're our girl, the way

Zack is our boy, and nothing will ever alter that."

Mentally her fingers were crossed. It never did to challenge fate, but in this case what choice did she have?

Cheryl sniffed wetly.

"Are you sure? Does that mean I don't have to finish in the garden? It's 'Tracey Beaker' on television soon and I want to watch that."

Somewhere deep down, Olwyn was aware of a bubble of laughter, in which she recognised a hint of hysteria. But it was humour all the same and much of her recent tension drained magically away.

"That's fine," she told the child. "But why not pop in the shower first? I'll find you some fresh clothes."

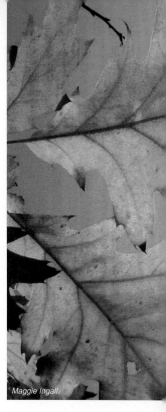

Maggie Ingall.

✳   ✳   ✳   ✳

She'd got away with it lightly, considering, Cheryl thought as she skipped down the drive. Zack was due to be dropped off at the gates and Mum had said she could go and meet him.

"Don't go wandering off, mind," had been her parting shot.

Reaching the gates, she glanced up and down the road. No car yet. She flopped down on one of the big white stones on the verge that stopped people from parking where they shouldn't, and sat watching the insects busy in the grass. After a while she grew bored.

Across the road was the wood that marked the boundary of the farm. It was a great place for climbing trees. Taking care not to go out of earshot of the road — it never did to flaunt the rules too much in one day — Cheryl wandered across to look for a likely candidate to climb.

Badgers rooted in the wood and Cheryl was poking curiously at a sett in the bank when she heard a sound, a snuffling, snorting sort of sound that made her freeze. Next moment there was a crashing in the undergrowth and who should emerge but Miranda!

"'Miranda! Oh, you bad girl! Where have you been?"

The huge Black Spot pig grunted and returned to the important business of foraging amongst the beech-mast and peaty ground. Finding a stout stick, Cheryl wielded it forcefully.

"Come on. Home!"

Zack turned up as they burst out of the wood.

"You've found her!" he cried. "Great! I've had an ace time. Andy's mum took us swimming. It was brilliant. How's your day been?"

"OK, but finding Miranda has definitely made it better." Cheryl gave him a grin. Surely Mum and Dad wouldn't cancel her birthday party now?

As they approached the farm, Miranda, catching the squeals of her field mates, answered them gleefully and set off at a rate of knots to join them.

Gold

S O many shades of
autumn, caught
On just one leafy bough —
As many shades of golden
As a palette will allow,
And who could not admire
  the skill
That paints this work of art,
Inspiring every spirit and
Uplifting every heart.
Those shapes and
  vibrant colours
No mortal could invoke,
For nature paints
  her pictures
With magic in each stroke.

— *Maggie Ingall.*

"T HERE goes Miranda!" Dad hollered from the garden. He brandished his fork in triumph and went to open the gate to the pig pasture. The pigs squealed all the louder, bringing Mum hastening from the house to see what the din was about. It was a momentous homecoming.

"What a clever girl to have found her like that," Mum remarked, smiling at Cheryl.

Dad nodded in agreement. Both were smiling happily. They looked altogether chummy again, just as they used to, and Cheryl's heart gave a little bump of hope.

"We've got some news for you," Dad said. "Remember us explaining how we were going to adopt you and make you officially ours? Like Zack?"

Cheryl nodded and rubbed a grimy hand across her face, leaving a smudge.

"Well, Mum and I rang the people in charge of the adoption this afternoon. And what do you think?"

"They said I could still have my birthday party?"

"No!" Both parents' faces crumpled. Cheryl looked from one to the other, not sure if they were about to laugh or cry.

"What I was trying to tell you is that the adoption has been finalised. You're our girl totally. Isn't it great?" Dad said.

"Great," Cheryl agreed. Mum had assured her that she was anyway, so she couldn't see what all the fuss was about. She was more concerned about her birthday. "Does this mean my birthday party is still on, then?"

The couple exchanged a puzzled glance and hugged Cheryl happily.

"Darling, of course it is. Whatever made you think otherwise?" Mum asked.

"Well, that time Zack messed around with the tractor, Dad stopped his pocket money. I thought I might be in for it, too."

"Not this time, Cheryl." Dad's deep-throated chuckle was telling. "And certainly not on your birthday. The very idea!"

Which just went to show, sister and brother agreed later, that there really was no accounting for the logic of grown-ups! ∎

Come To The Fair

THIS time, Saul Hatton was in two minds whether to attend the fair at Widecombe. It fell in mid-September, a busy period for him, what with minds turning to winter snows and folks wanting new clogs to see them safely over the treacherous roads and tracks.

On the other hand, Widecombe Fair always brought him a choice bit of trade. Last year he had taken on a booth, and sold more clogs than he'd thought possible to buyers from all across the moor.

It was where he'd met Hannie. At the thought of the girl from Manaton, a hamlet three miles to the north east, Saul's hand stilled over the lathe.

Hannie Merriday was as blithe and bonnie as her name suggested. Her ready smile, flashing blue eyes and tangle of brown hair that tossed about her as she danced held her audience captive.

She made the daintiest picture it was possible to make, and Saul, watching the step-dancing competition, had been as entranced as the rest.

Unfortunately for Hannie, she didn't win and when she jumped breathlessly down from the staging in a flurry of white petticoats, Saul could see why.

On her feet she wore not the lightweight clogs of the step-dancer, but the plain, everyday sort a girl might use to tramp to market or work in the fields; heavy and cumbersome.

"Well, then, maid," he heard himself blurt out, "if that wasn't the tidiest bit of dancing I've ever seen."

"Why, thank you." She shot him a blushing, regretful smile. Her eyes were harebell blue. "I wish I could have carried on, but my feet went like lead and I couldn't keep it up any more."

Everyone knew the rules. The competitor who could keep going the longest

by Pauline
Kelly.

came off the winner
— in today's case a
lass from Princetown,
wearing the lightest
pair of step-clogs money
could buy.

"It's no surprise you felt
tired," Saul exclaimed. "You need the right footwear for the game, maid. Your
feet wouldn't let you down then."

His advice was kindly meant, and she smiled again, a little winsomely,
before moving on.

That was all it took. From that moment, Saul was besotted.

As the day progressed the ox was roasted, the cider flowed and the fiddler,
by now well into his cups, played for the dancing like one possessed. Hannie
was there amongst them, dancing her very best.

Saul couldn't take his eyes off her.

"Pretty wench, isn't she?" a voice said at his side.

Thomas Dodd, the Widecombe blacksmith, knew all there was to know
hereabouts.

"Her da's a miner from Manaton way. Six brothers, she's got; Hannie's the

109

only girl, so it'll fall on her to help her ma in the house. Why don't you ask her to dance?"

"What, me? Two left feet I've got, and that's a fact."

Saul could no more step in time to the rhythm than fly to the moon. His talent lay in his workshop, fashioning clogs to fit to perfection, helping tiny feet grow straight and strong, keeping older feet snug and dry and never, ever chafing.

Make strictly to measure was Saul's rule of thumb. A pattern was drawn of a customer's foot, and the precious sheets of paper carefully stored on a shelf above his bench.

He realised Thomas was speaking.

"If it's a wife you're after, you won't get better than Hannie. The Merridays are a decent, God-fearing family. Hannie will have been shown how to cook and how to keep a tidy hearth.

"Mark you," Thomas continued airily, "I favour the bachelor existence myself — you can please yourself then. Have you noticed how you can always pick out a married man? Henpecked, he looks. Never a moment to call his own, always having to mend this shelf or dig that patch of ground, the poor browbeaten fool. Women? You can keep them!"

Saul did not entirely agree with this philosophy. It seemed to him that a wife to share a fellow's life, with maybe one or two little ones at her knee, was no bad thing.

Back at the cottage that had been built by his grandfather, the founder of the business, Saul went straight up to bed, but not to sleep. An image of dancing feet and tossing brown hair played on his senses.

Over at Clapper Bridge lived a widow he had been meaning to call on. He knew now he never would.

✳   ✳   ✳   ✳

Reflectively, Saul picked up the clog he'd been shaping and began to hollow out the instep. After that day, whenever he had gone into Ashburton for supplies, he had looked out for Hannie and her mother in the market place, and often paused to pass the time of day.

The last time had been in June, when for once Hannie was on her own. She wore a flimsy shawl over her harebell-blue gown, and tucked into the brim of her straw bonnet was a posy of harebells. She looked as charming as the day.

"No Mama today?" Saul lifted his cap in greeting. "I trust she's not poorly?"

"Dear me, no. Mother's in good health, thank you. It's the glove making, you know." Many a village woman made gloves for a supplier in Tavistock to help make ends meet. "What with one thing and another, the glove work has fallen behind."

"So you're doing the shopping while your mama catches up." Saul eyed the laden baskets in her hands.

"You've a long walk ahead of you. Can I . . . may I offer you a lift in the cart?"

Hannie's round face coloured up prettily.

"Oh, but I couldn't! Manaton is out of your way."

"No matter." Saul would have driven three times round Dartmoor for the chance of having Hannie on the seat beside him. "The horse will be rested, and he'll make nothing of the extra miles. Are you nearly finished here?"

"Just about. I need some cottons and one or two other things, then I'm done."

"Then let me hold your baskets while you fetch them."

SHE went tripping off, despite the clumpish workaday clogs she still wore. While she was gone, Saul picked up some items for himself; a wedge of good hard cheese from the produce stall, a box of tin tacks from the ironmonger.

All the time he kept in sight Hannie's flower-decked bonnet, bobbing in and out of the crowd. The harebells were beginning to wilt, and suddenly Saul wanted to treat her to some silk flowers that would last from one of the stalls. Or else some coloured ribbons for her hair, or maybe a sugar plum — any small token that would bring the stars to her eyes just for him.

It was a simple gesture that any village youth would have made in a trice, but the crippling shyness that overcame Saul where womenfolk were concerned had him in its grip. All he could do was stand helplessly by and wait for Hannie to complete her list of requirements.

A little while later, he was clambering up beside her on the cart, and behind them, the day's purchases joggled cheerfully as they rumbled along.

"Do you always do your own shopping, Saul?" Hannie enquired chattily. "I can't see my da managing it. He wouldn't know what to get."

"Perhaps he's never had to see after himself. Me, I live very simply. A bite of bread and cheese, and I'm happy."

"Bread and cheese?" Hannie shook her head sagely. "That's men for you. Don't you ever wish for a hot beef stew and dumplings?"

"Aye, but after a long day's work I don't wish to make it."

"But, Saul, you prepare the food beforehand. You put the pot over the flame and let it cook slowly throughout the day. Then it's all ready and waiting for you at suppertime."

"I tried that once." Saul gave the reins a twitch.

"And?"

"I went in to charred remains and a ruined pot. Didn't get rid of the stink for days."

Hannie pealed with good-natured laughter.

"You had the fire too fierce, you goose! You need to tamp it down. And always make sure there's plenty of liquid in the pot."

"Reckon I'm best making do with bread and cheese," Saul growled, but he was smiling. It was impossible to be out of sorts with Hannie.

Eventually they reached Manaton, a pretty hamlet of stone-built dwellings flanking a sheep-cropped green, and as he pulled up outside the Merridew cottage, Saul's heart sank. What girl in her right mind would want to exchange a good stout Devon stone house roofed with slate for his flimsy cob and thatch affair?

Everything was against him! Saul's farewell, when Hannie clambered lightly down from the cart, was more curt than he intended. Handing over her the shopping baskets, he shook up the horse and went clattering away.

Meeting Hannie, he'd decided, was only adding to his agony. He'd avoided the market ever since.

When Thomas Dodd had enquired if he had given any more thought to Hannie Merriday, Saul had given his head a decisive shake and left it at that.

He began to sing as he worked. Plain of face and awkward in manner he might be, but Saul was possessed of a fine bass voice that helped to pass many a long hour at his workbench, never more so than now. It was a fine, sunny day and his song rang out through the open doorway, bringing a smile to the faces of passers-by.

In the forge a few doors along, Thomas, repairing a broken ploughshare, listened thoughtfully for a few moments. Then he put aside his work and headed for the clog-maker's shop.

"Morning, Saul. Wonder if I could have a word?"

"Don't tell me those new clogs have worn through already?"

"No, it isn't that. It was your singing. It put me in mind of my quartet."

Thomas's popular group of songsters, who entertained robustly at the Hare and Hart on a Saturday night and with slightly more decorum at Matins the next morning, were invariably called upon to perform at public functions. Widecombe Fair would not have been the same without the hearty country voices chiming out the well-known saga of Tom Pearce and his friends.

"Oh? And why would that be, Thomas?" Saul was beginning to feel faintly uneasy.

"I wondered if you'd act as stand-in if need be? Tenors and baritones are ten-a-penny, but finding a good bass is like looking for snow in June. I've been meaning to ask you for a while."

Saul deliberated. He was used to singing a solo part in church and occasionally, sufficiently mellowed with cider, he could be called upon to give a song at the alehouse. No. It was the thought of those public occasions that irked.

"Fair day's coming up. I was giving it a miss this time," he said.

"Not attend the fair?" Thomas looked shocked. "Man, what's got into you? Everyone will be there."

That was the trouble — everyone including Hannie. He'd have to watch her dance with all those fellows bold enough to claim her. He'd have to watch her laugh with them, chat to them, even indulge in a little harmless flirting, while he stood by powerless to join in the fun.

"'Tisn't obligatory that you should be there," Thomas pressed. "Year after

Ballachulish And Loch Leven, Scotland

*A*S a fervent film buff, I was determined to go to see where much of "Highlander 1 and 3", "Braveheart" and "Rob Roy" had been filmed. I finally managed it three years ago, and had a wonderful holiday, even if the weather wasn't always ideal. It's the perfect spot for experiencing the breathtaking scenery of Glencoe, on the shores of Loch Leven.

Whenever I walk down the street in my town and see all the slate roofs on the houses, I get a thrill to know I've been to the place they probably came from.

— *M.S., Elm Park.*

J. CAMPBELL KERR.

year the men have turned up to sing. All I'm asking is if you're interested?"

"I'll think about it," Saul said.

"Right-oh. By the way . . ." Thomas paused. "It's come to my notice that the Merridays have fallen on hard times. Not that it's your concern."

Saul was still for a moment.

"No," he acknowledged shortly.

THOMAS'S words played on Saul's mind. What had he meant? Was Hannie in some sort of danger? He had to find out.

Not having attended the market in weeks he was pitifully low on supplies, so on market day he set aside his reservations, hitched up the horse and trotted to Ashburton, rehearsing how he would greet Hannie if he happened to bump into her and what excuse he would give for his absence.

All at once, the very prospect of seeing her again was sweet.

He stabled the horse at the inn, headed for the market place and made his purchases.

There was no sign of Hannie or her mother, and although he hung around for the greater part of the morning, they still did not turn up. In the end he asked the woman on the haberdashers' stall if she could help.

"Hannie Merriday?" The woman threw up her hands in surprise. "Haven't you heard? Her poor father met with an accident at the tin mine and broke his arm."

"I didn't know. Will he be all right?"

"Seems so, given a few weeks. With him laid off for the time being and no money coming in, Hannie's joined her ma at the glove making. Well, every bit helps." The woman looked Saul over shrewdly.

"Was there something special you wanted to see her about?"

"Um . . . not really. Will she be at the fair, do you know?"

"I should say so!" The stallholder folded her arms emphatically. "There's been a donation of five golden sovereigns for the winner of the step-dancing competition. Five pounds would go a long way for the Merridays. If Hannie wins, it'll lighten their load a lot. If you get my meaning."

"Indeed," Saul said. "I understand you very clearly."

As he left the market place, his mind raced. How did Hannie stand a chance of victory in worn old clogs? The clog-maker here at Ashburton was, in Saul's opinion, high on prices and low on workmanship. If Hannie was to achieve her aim, Saul must see to it himself.

Feeling more positive, he went home again.

In the barn behind his cottage, he kept his raw materials. Saul always bought the wood in the green and seasoned it himself — that way there was never a problem with the clogs splitting.

Rejecting a section of beech that was more suited to the sturdier Morris dancing, he found what he was looking for — a perfect length of ash, light and springy, which would give a good ring against the wooden boards of the platform as the dancer performed the steps.

As he carried the items into the workshop, Saul pondered over what sort of decoration to fashion. Scrolled clogs took longer to make than plain. Great skill went into the patterning, not that Saul was bothered. These clogs had to be his very best.

One thing only troubled him — he had no pattern of Hannie's foot, but years of experience and a careful eye paid off.

First Saul had to honour his existing orders. All the next week, from dawn till dusk, the rasp and hammer of the clog-maker's tools rang out relentlessly. Saul barely allowed himself space to eat before he was back at his bench.

When at last the orders were done and duly delivered, Saul realised it was almost upon him and he had not yet started on those special dancing clogs.

He began the task at once, cutting and shaping, and when darkness fell he continued in the glow of a lamp. By the early hours of the day of the fair, the clogs were done. Tenderly he threaded the holes with extra fine laces, polished the leather uppers to a fine gleam.

Magic had entered his fingers as he plied his craft. Saul held the clogs up in the yellow beam of the lamp so that the pattern of harebells stood out clearly, and knew he had achieved his aim. Now to get them to the wearer.

Deciding against taking the horse, whose rowdy clatter would wake the soundest sleeper, he made the long miles to Manaton on foot. After leaving his gift outside the Merridays' cottage, he trudged home again. The eastern sky was lightening to dawn when he fell, fully clothed, on to his bed and slept.

Not long afterwards, he was wakened by an urgent hammering on the door. Yawning and bleary-eyed, he answered the summons and found Thomas on the step, his leathery face working anxiously.

"Saul, man. I've a problem. Remember my asking you about the quartet?"

Saul clapped his hand to his brow.

"'Sakes, I've been that busy it went right out of my mind."

"No matter. You know Carter Bostock, who sings bass? Not the voice you've got, mind, but adequate. He's had to go off to Wiltshire and won't be back in time for the fair. Could you take his place?"

"What, now?"

"You can do it, Saul. You know the songs, you're a dab hand at harmony. If you say no, we're sunk."

Thomas gave a desperate sigh, and Saul's heart softened.

"Let me have a wash and brush up," he told the smith. "I'll be with you shortly."

*   *   *   *

On the outskirts of Widecombe the fair was in full swing. Saul had played his part, and their final song had been received with characteristic enthusiasm, the onlookers joining in gustily with the chorus.

"Wi' Bill Brewer, Jan Stewer, Peter Gurney, Peter Davey, Dan'l Whiddon,

'Arry 'Awk, Old Uncle Tom Cobley and all. Old Uncle Tom Cobley and all."

Saul, still singing the words, threaded his way between the booths of tempting home-made produce, fairings and cheap lace, past the roll-a-penny stall that attracted children and adults alike. He was making for the step-dancing platform.

Amongst the competitors, supremely confident, was last year's winner, but Saul had eyes only for Hannie. She had trimmed up her plain blue gown with bands of coloured braid, and tied back her hair with ribbon. She looked both apprehensive and excited.

Peeping beneath the hem of her skirt were the toes of the dancing clogs he had sat up half the night making.

"And now, ladies and gentlemen," the Master of Ceremonies roared, "let's give a big welcome to the maids who are going to dance for us. When you're ready, fiddler!"

A great round of applause pulled the first girl on to the stage. The fiddler started with a merry jig and the competition began, fast and furious.

Supping a tankard of cider, Saul watched with joy as Hannie won the event, to a delighted roar. He saw her awarded the prize of five gleaming sovereigns, then turned away and headed for the exit.

Step Bac

The Wallace Monument

IN 1869, almost six hundred years after William Wallace's astonishing victory against the English at the Battle of Stirling Bridge, the final stones of the National Wallace Monument were eased into place.

The tower is situated just outside Stirling on Abbey Craig — the hill from which Wallace reportedly watched the advancing English on September 11, 1297.

Inside the monument is an exhibition detailing the life and times of the Scottish hero from his early life to the trial that condemned him to death.

Wallace's famous

When he was almost there, a hand tugged at his sleeve. Looking down, he saw Hannie, very out of breath, highly indignant.

"Saul Hatton! What do you mean by running off like this? I wanted to thank you." She looked at him earnestly. "'Twas you left the clogs, wasn't it?"

"Aye. I'm glad you won, Hannie."

"All due to you! These are the most wonderful clogs I've ever had."

"That's good to hear. I wish you luck, maid. I hope one day you find some lad who'll take you dancing and make you happy."

He made to go, but she pulled him back.

"Take me dancing? Why, you great goose! What would I want with that? Someone to sing to me, now . . ." Hannie slanted a sideways look, mischievous, provocative. "A voice that slips and slithers around a girl's senses like dark honey — that's what I dream of."

Saul swallowed hard.

"It is? Hannie, maid . . . seems to me a fellow needs more to offer a girl to

116

_PA._

broadsword is on display here with its impressive fifty-two-inch blade.

To handle such a weapon, Wallace would

_PA._

have needed to be at least six feet six inches tall — amazing considering the average height of the time was just five feet.

Wallace isn't the only Scottish person to be celebrated here, however. The monument boasts a Hall of Heroes with marble busts of some of Scotland's best-loved children. ∎

keep her content than a song or two. She needs a decent house to be mistress of —"

"What better than one made of cob, and roofed with golden thatch? Especially when it's kept so trim that the walls shine in the sun. Especially when her man's right there on the other side of that wall, working at his bench, and not down some dark old tin mine with danger at every turn." Her voice quivered with emotion.

Saul, recalling the catastrophe that had wrought such havoc in her family and could have ended in tragedy, wanted to take her in his arms and comfort her.

"I don't know what to say, Hannie. I'm not good with words."

"It's no great worry. I can talk enough for two."

"I can well believe it," Saul mumbled. "Hannie?"

"Yes?"

"Could we . . ." He moistened his dry lips. "Could we walk out together, d'you think?"

"Well, Saul Hatton! Didn't I just hear something about being no good with words?"

"Aye, you did."

"Those are the most glorious words I've ever heard," she whispered, eyes shining. "And yes, I'd be glad to walk out with you. Shall we start with a look round the fair? I was in such a tizzy over the dancing I couldn't give it a thought before . . ."

Beaming joyfully down at her, Saul took her hand in his and guided her back towards the throngs of revellers. He was proud of his girl in her pretty gown and stylish new clogs — the best he had ever made.

Thomas Dodd watched them go. He was smiling. The five sovereigns he had forked out for the prize money had been well worth the sacrifice. He'd taken a chance on Saul rising to the occasion over the fancy footwear — but he knew his friend. Never one to turn his back on those in need, particularly when he was so obviously taken with the girl anyway.

Of course, it had been a different matter persuading Carter Bostock to stand down as bass for once. Near half a barrel of ale it had taken to achieve it! He'd bet a pound to a penny the man was abed yet, nursing a sore head!

All's well that ends well, Thomas thought. It was grand to see the young couple together. Matchmaking mightn't be his strong point, but it had worked this time, thanks to Widecombe Fair! ∎

Puppy

I WAKE early to the sound of the dawn chorus and, in between that instant of dreaming and waking, I experience a sense of dislocation. Then it comes to me.

Today, my life is going to change for ever. It is a strange sensation. I lie listening to the tranquillity of birdsong and it seems so at odds with my growing panic.

Am I really doing the right thing? I stretch and yawn, the sound alerting my dog to my waking. I hear his soft padding in the hallway. Then he's nosing open the bedroom door.

"Good morning, Pirate."

He wags his tail and thrusts his warm muzzle into my outstretched fingers. It is solid and reassuring.

And it's then that I smile.

* * * *

"That dog's following us," I said to my friend, Andrea.

We were walking slowly and the dog slower still. It was limping and every so often it would stop and sit.

"It's probably a farm dog."

I stopped and turned. It wore no collar and its brown-and-white coat looked dusty, as if it had been rolling in the sun-baked earth.

"Here, boy, here, boy," I said, clapping my thigh.

The dog hesitated as a car, kicking up dust, came slowly along the rutted lane, spoiling the moment. By the time the car had passed and the dust clouds had settled, the dog had disappeared.

We continued on our walk with Andrea telling me about her daughter's forthcoming wedding.

I listened, having no contribution of my own. Lately my life had seemed flat, awash with a watercolour of grey, and Andrea I knew wasn't interested in work talk, even though we were colleagues in a multi-national company.

"Isn't twenty really young to be getting married these days?" I finally asked.

"Giselle, Linzie's known him for years!" Andrea exclaimed, casting me a sideways look. "Besides, not everyone is like you, you know."

"You mean cautious?"

Power!

by Mhairi Grant.

Illustration by
David Axtell.

"Did I say that?" she asked, throwing me an impish smile.

But she didn't need to. I knew what Andrea thought. At thirty-five I had let opportunities in my personal life slip by almost unnoticed.

"Been too fussy," was what Andrea had said.

But I liked my own company and living alone. And I used to work long hours. Used to, but not now.

"Actually," my friend continued, "I would say stupid more than cautious — especially when it comes to Brad."

I frowned.

"Brad and I argued too much."

"I liked him," she said for the umpteenth time since Brad and I had gone our separate ways. "He had the measure of you, my lady, and he had his head screwed on."

I used to think that I had my head screwed on as well and it had come as a shock when the doctor had told me that I was suffering from stress.

People like me didn't suffer from stress — or so I thought. For the first time ever I was taking sick leave from my job.

And it was giving me a different perspective on things.

But not on Brad — he was history. Why Andrea kept on and on about him beat me.

"Drop it, Andrea," I muttered, feeling uncomfortable whenever the subject of my ex-boyfriend came up.

"But he was —"

"Andrea!" I growled in mock warning. "You'll be going for a walk alone in future if you don't change the subject!"

IN the end, she did drop the subject and we continued on our way. But the next day I went for a walk alone — because Andrea was at work.

Walking was one of my newly discovered joys and I hummed quietly as I surveyed the road ahead.

I had a backpack with some water and a ham sandwich in it, together with a map. I liked the sense of purpose it gave me. It made me feel like a real walker.

Two miles into the walk I came upon paths in the woods going off in different directions. I stopped to consult the map. It was then that I saw the dog.

It was sitting back in the trees looking at me. I had never owned an animal and had no intention of doing so but . . . something gave me pause. I got out my sandwich, tore a bit off and offered it to the dog.

It came towards me, stooping low, its tail between its legs. I noticed a bald patch on its neck as if a collar or rope had rubbed the hair away.

"I won't hurt you," I murmured, dropping the sandwich where the dog could get it without having to touch me.

I doubt the animal even tasted it, he snapped it up so fast. In the end he ate the whole thing.

✱　　✱　　✱　　✱

"I think the animal is a stray," I said over the phone to the RSPCA later in the day. "It's certainly neglected and followed me home from my walk."

And now it was outside, making me regret my earlier decision. I hated to see animals suffer but I had no intention of letting it into the house.

I peeped out the window. He lay with his head on his paws, watching the front door.

"I have no idea what type of dog it is," I replied in response to the woman's question. "But it is brown and white with a patch over one eye."

There, I had done my duty.

But the RSPCA couldn't find it. I was perplexed and so were they. Twice I called them and each time the dog had disappeared. I mentioned it to Andrea when she popped in with Linzie's wedding invitation.

"If it shows up again, why not keep it?"

"It's not fair to keep a dog when I'm working full-time."

"Phone Brad, he may be able to find a home for it."

Brad was a vet so it was inevitable that his name crop up in relation to the dog but still, I hoped that the dog would go away.

It didn't. In the end, I started to feed it. I think it slept under the shed in the garden but I didn't go out to investigate. I didn't want to know.

Yet, at night in bed I would lie awake, staring into the darkness and thinking about the dog. And once, just on the edge of sleep, my tears leaked out on to the pillow at the thought of it being abandoned.

THE next day I let it into the house.

"And don't think that you're staying here for good," I stated. "This is just an interim measure."

Or so I had led myself to believe. But one look into his eyes and I knew that I was sinking. I went out to the shops and bought dog food. A week later, I was in the pet shop to get bedding and a collar and lead. By then I had resigned myself to the inevitable.

"You'll have to get Pirate checked over," one of my doggy pals had said. "You know, make sure he gets his injections."

"But what if someone claims him?" I asked, making one last protest.

I knew that no-one was going to claim him.

I'd tried everything — pinning posters on trees, a notice in the newsagent's . . . I even took out an advert in the local paper, but still no-one claimed him.

Besides, Pirate and I got on so well. He was house-trained and lovable.

We got into a routine. In the mornings after breakfast we'd go for a walk in the woods. Lunchtime it was the local park and in the evening, wherever the fancy took us.

The grey of my life began to lift but there was still an absence. It was like going into a family room and finding books left open, the table set and CDs scattered over the floor but nobody there. It was the lack of noise. My life was a silent one, broken only by Pirate's occasional bark.

Eventually I bowed to the inevitable and took Pirate to Brad. He was the only local vet and Pirate was still favouring a back leg.

I had only spoken to the receptionist and Brad was unprepared when he saw me in the waiting-room. I, too, was a bundle of nerves.

The last time I had seen him, we had had a terrible argument.

Brad was always running late — his appointments at his surgery only ran on time because of his receptionist.

We had tickets for the theatre and I had so been looking forward to the performance, but, as usual, Brad had turned up late.

Willie Shand.

"A dog had been run over," he'd said. "What was I to do? Leave it to bleed to death?"

"You could have telephoned."

"I forgot — I had to operate immediately to save the dog's life."

Due to my own work commitments, we had been seeing so little of each other, and that evening had been the last straw.

Now, as I looked at him, I couldn't for the life of me keep the wobble out of my voice. He looked so thin and harried.

"So, boy, what have you been up to, eh?" he asked as I explained the circumstances.

I watched as he looked over Pirate. He checked his teeth.

"He's a young dog. About two years old, I would say."

He ran his hands over Pirate's body, paying particular attention to his pelvis. For some reason I couldn't help but look at his hands. I had never seen Brad at work before and it fascinated me. He really was a gentle, caring man.

"I think we'll need an X-ray . . ." his voice interrupted my thoughts.

I nodded. I could cope with Brad in his professional mode, but on the way out he put a hand on my arm.

122

A Stitch In Time

MOTHER NATURE'S thread of
gold will sew an autumn scene,
Where falling leaves will carpet what
so recently was green,
She'll bead the winter berries on the
hedgerows as they bud,
And weave the sparkling streams
as summer trickle becomes flood.

Then as darkness falls and stars
cascade across the sky,
Frosty web will drift and cover
hedgerows, by and by.
Hibernating creatures will soon
disappear to sleep,
While, noses upon windows, cosy
children come to peep.

Watching over all will be a rising
hunter's moon,
Sailing the horizon like a dawning
sun in June.
Tapestry complete, we'll thank the
Lord for what we see,
For summer beauty past and winter
splendour yet to be.

— *Pam Davies.*

"How have you been, Giselle?"

"Fine. I'm walking more, trying to keep fit."

"I hear that you're off work."

"I'll be back soon," I replied, not wanting to elaborate. "So, Pirate's to get another injection and an X-ray . . ."

As I walked out of the door I felt Brad watching me. Don't turn round, don't turn round.

But when I stopped to open the car door, I couldn't help but look. Brad was standing, hands in pockets, and at that moment, he looked as abandoned as Pirate had been. It was then that I felt something inside me give way. Like a cliff, after years of erosion, falling into the sea. I scrambled into the car and gunned the engine, trying to put as much distance as possible between us.

I'M not the crying type, but that night I cried. I cried so hard that Pirate came up to me and licked my tears. I hugged him.

Brad had said that there was a lot of collie and some Alsatian in him but at that moment, to me, he was just a warm, breathing animal who cared.

Brad had cared as well. I knew that now. Even though, for fear of being hurt, I had tried to keep him from getting too close.

But I was hurt anyway. In fact, inside I felt like dying. I had missed Brad so much. I knew that now. It wasn't so much stress brought on by my job but the fact that . . . I loved Brad — I always had. How could I have been so stupid?

Brad had tried so many times to tell me that I was driving him away but I wouldn't listen. Yet, he hadn't quite given up on me even as he had walked out my door for the last time.

"If you ever change your mind about us, give me a call. I'll be waiting for you."

The memory brought fresh tears. It was late by the time I roused myself from the settee. I hadn't eaten or even taken Pirate for his evening walk. He looked at me with soulful eyes.

"In a minute, boy," I murmured, going to the drawer.

I took out Linzie's wedding invitation. The invite was to Giselle Hammond and partner — it was as good an excuse as any.

I had planned what I was going to say, rehearsed it in my mind as I took Pirate for his walk.

I would phone Brad and ask him to be my partner. But it didn't work out like that.

Pirate and I soon found ourselves in a different part of town, right in front of Brad's house. I can't even remember getting there. I felt drained and exhilarated; bold and terrified and, above all, a burning need to make amends — to make things right between us.

When I rang the doorbell, Brad did more than open the door — he opened his arms as well.

There was no need for my carefully rehearsed words. As I walked into his arms it was as if it was meant to be.

"I love you," I murmured. "I always have."

"Giselle . . .!" he cried, lifting me off my feet. "You don't know how much I have dreamed of you saying that."

As we kissed, Pirate started to bark and run frantically round our feet, as if saying, *What about me? What about me?* Eventually we looked down at him.

"Do you think I've got a problem dog on my hands?" I asked as we knelt down to pet him.

"A jealous one, I would say. But don't worry, I'll win him over. It should be a piece of cake, after you."

I punched him playfully on the arm and we laughed as Pirate insinuated himself between us and went all sloppy on us.

* * * *

"Brad did win you over, didn't he, Pirate?" I say now, scratching his ears.

At the mention of Brad's name, Pirate gives a soft whine. He adores Brad. I get out of bed and go to the window. It is a beautiful day — a day for weddings. I head for the shower, but before I get there, the phone rings.

"Hello, Gorgeous. How are you feeling?"

"On top of the world," I reply, unable to keep the smile out of my voice.

"Not getting cold feet?"

"No, I'm looking forward to it."

"Well, I'm getting cold feet. I'm not sure there's a need for all this marriage business, do you?"

"Listen, Buster," I reply with mock severity, "you'd better get to the church on time or I'll set my hound on you."

"That wouldn't look good, not in my profession. I suppose I had better turn up."

"I'll be waiting for you."

Who would have thought it? I'm actually going to marry Brad. It's then that I realise that I can hardly wait . . . ■

A T the age of fifteen I planned to marry Donny Osmond.
I'd imagined it all in detail — I'd be in the front row at a concert, he'd be singing "Puppy Love".

"Someone help me, help me, help me please!" he'd agonise, moving along the stage singing to his fans. Then he'd see me, and something would connect between us. After the concert one of his people would single me out and call me backstage. The following day I'd be invited to his hotel where we'd have a romantic dinner followed by a passionate kiss.

"I have to tell the world that I'm going to marry you," he'd whisper in my ear.

He's The One!

by Susan Sarapuk.

Illustration by Mark Viney.

125

The next day it would be all over the papers: *The Girl Who Broke A Million Hearts!*

Everyone in school would be madly jealous, and of course, that would be the end of my school days. I'd be whisked off to America, where we'd have a huge, lavish wedding and then live happily ever after.

I recounted this every day to my best friend, Alice, as we waited for the school bus. She put up with my bagging Donny because she preferred his brother, Jay.

"But when are we going to get to one of their concerts?" she'd point out unhelpfully. "They're always in London."

She was right. And my parents would never let me go to one, however much I begged.

"We can't afford it!"

"What's all this nonsense about pop groups anyway!" My dad would glance over the top of his paper. "All long hair and noise — I can't understand you girls screaming at them."

There were a lot of things my dad couldn't understand.

"Don't you worry, he'll realise Donny and I were made for each other," I told Alice confidently.

I used to watch their shows on TV willing Donny to connect with me through the screen (not realising that they were all pre-recorded). And afterwards I'd retire to my room, playing their records and drooling over their posters.

We girls competed with one another in school over who was the Osmonds' greatest fan.

"I've got more posters than you!"

"I've got the latest badge!"

"I get 'Osmonds' World' every month!" Well, didn't we all!

Anyway, I knew I was Donny's greatest fan, because — unlike the rest of them — I was going to marry him.

DONNY had his detractors, of course. There were the David Cassidy fans. But how could you compare the two? I used to say that David Cassidy was insipid. I liked the word, and enjoyed using it a lot because it infuriated the Cassidy-ites.

Worse than those were the boys who were into progressive rock, like Alastair Newton. He loved to make fun of me.

"The Who are the greatest band in the world!" he'd sneer. I just thought he was a saddo; obviously jealous of Donny. I bet he would have liked to have millions of girls screaming for him, but it was never going to happen. I doubted he'd ever get a girlfriend.

"Maybe we could go to America?" Alice said one day in Domestic Science over the bowls of ingredients we were supposed to be stirring. I was the world's worst cook, and I knew my pineapple turnover would be a disaster. Some of my classmates were already putting theirs into the oven, but Alice and I tended to loiter and chatter. Mrs Hyde, in her overall and pearls and overpowering perfume (which we all knew she wore to impress the Woodwork teacher), bustled up and tutted.

"Come on, girls! Stop talking!"

"You mean fly on a plane?" I turned the muck in my bowl out on to the baking tin. "Won't that cost a lot of money? Plus, we're only fifteen; we can't go on our own."

"But next year we'll be sixteen! And, if we start saving now . . ."

Suddenly I was excited.

"We could find out where they live in Utah!"

Donny wouldn't have to search me out in a crowd after all — not if I turned up on his doorstep.

"Girls, are you listening to a word I say?" Mrs Hyde screeched.

Obviously not! We carried on our discussion at the end of the lesson.

"Of course, we'll have to earn some money," Alice said. "Pocket money won't go far."

"I'll get a paper round."

WE announced it to the class the following day as if it were already an accomplished fact. Soon it was around the school.

"Jen and Alice are going to America to see the Osmonds next year!"

We were minor celebrities, fêted and held in awe. I lapped it up; besides, I'd better get used to it if I was going to marry Donny.

My parents were impressed over my new enthusiasm for work. I offered to do more around the house and garden — for payment. I didn't tell them what I was saving for — that was a subject that would need to be broached at the right time, even I knew that.

The paper round wasn't much fun, mind, especially on wet, dark mornings.

"Just think of your true love," I told myself in the gloomy newsagent's. "You'll be sweet sixteen when you meet, the perfect age."

"Hi. I think this is one of yours. It got into my bag by mistake."

I looked up from my daydreaming to see a lanky boy with long hair falling into his eyes. He was wearing flares and a chocolate brown leather jacket, and held out a copy of the "Daily Mirror". It was marked *26, Norton Avenue*.

"Well, I've just finished!" I said, exasperated. "I'm not going back. You should deliver it — it's your fault!"

He shrugged, and dumped it on the counter.

"Your job," he said and then walked away and jumped on his bike.

Of course, I had to deliver it. I didn't want the sack and I needed the money.

"So you're the girl who's going to marry Donny Osmond," he said the next time our paths crossed.

"I suppose you think the Osmonds are rubbish," I challenged him.

"'Crazy Horses' was good'," he answered. "At least they're musicians."

At last! I glowed with pride.

"They're brilliant!" I declared.

"I wouldn't go that far."

"Who do you like, then?"

"Dylan, the Moody Blues."

I sniffed dismissively.

"Have you ever listened to them?" he asked.

"No."

He grinned.

"I'll lend you some records."

"I don't even know your name."

"Chris."

"I'm Jen. You don't go to my school," I said, stating the obvious.

"No, I go to the old St Joseph's Grammar on the other side of town."

CHRIS brought me his records. I wasn't impressed with them. Every morning I brought one back, and he'd discuss its merits with me outside the newsagent. Discuss? Argue, more like. No-one was better than my beloved Osmonds! But Chris just called me a philistine. I didn't know what he meant.

"All right, give me one of yours," he said one day.

I gave him "The Plan", telling him to guard it with his life. For all I knew, he could be chummy with Alastair Newton, trying to get his hands on my stuff to destroy it. That Alastair Newton would go to any lengths!

"Not bad," he admitted when he brought it back the following day.

Alice wasn't that excited when I told her we might have made a male convert.

"Boys are all right, really." She blushed. "Larry Lambert — he's nice, isn't he?"

Larry Lambert, hulking rugby player in 5R? Come to think of it, Alice had been acting all giggly around him. Now she began to talk about him a lot — a bit too much, if you asked me.

When I wanted to discuss whether Donny would mind that I wasn't a Mormon, or if I should perhaps convert now, she frowned.

"Larry is C of E and I'm Baptist, do you think that matters?"

I gave up. I was a bit worried that she was losing her focus.

"The fair's coming next week," Chris told me that evening. "Do you want to come?"

"With you?"

"Yeah."

"OK." It was my turn to shrug.

I'd never really been out with a boy before — I was being loyal to Donny, naturally. But next year was a long way off.

It was nice to be with someone, to feel someone tall and protective at my side. To be just like Julie Fanshawe and Helen Rees who were always on the arms of their latest boyfriends and looked down on me with pity.

Chris held me when I screamed on the waltzers, and it was quite pleasant. He looked a bit like Donny, I thought, squinting at him sideways, with his dark hair and brown eyes and his leather jacket. I didn't know if he could sing, though! We had a laugh, and at the end of the night I felt warm inside.

"I like you," Chris said when we were in the shadow of the rifle range.

Then he kissed me. I struggled for breath, because it wasn't a bit like kissing my poster of Donny on the bedroom wall, and I was thrown by it.

"I didn't think it would be like that," I said stupidly, pulling away.

"Good, though, isn't it?" He grinned. And then he slipped his hand in mine and walked me home.

Kissing Chris would be good practice for when I met Donny, I decided. After all, I wouldn't want him to think I was a complete novice. In the end, the practice turned out to be really quite pleasant, and soon the paper round wasn't about saving money any more, but about meeting Chris.

ALICE and I reviewed our savings a couple of months later, tipping out our piggy banks on to her bedroom floor while Donny sang "The Twelfth Of Never".

"We haven't got enough. We'll never have enough!" she moaned.

"Maybe we could go the year after next?" I suggested tentatively.

She looked at me wide-eyed.

"But can you wait another year for Donny?"

"I'll have to."

"I think Larry's going to ask me to go on holiday with his family to the Norfolk Broads." Alice imported this information as if it was dynamite and I held the detonator. "I'll need my savings for that."

"We'll go to America the year after that." I said it again, as if saying it emphatically enough would make it happen. "We will!"

"Oh, yes, we will."

✳   ✳   ✳   ✳

We never did go, of course. And you might also have realised that I didn't marry Donny Osmond. I never even met him, although I did eventually get to a concert when I was a student and screamed my head off like a teenager again.

Chris often says, though, that he likes the Osmonds. After all, if it hadn't been for them, he and I might never have met and eventually married! ■

A Pair Of Size Seven Boots

by Mary Kettlewell.

IT was the rattle of kettle drums and the mouth organs we heard first. Then the steady tramp, tramp, tramp of cobbled boots.

Soon I could make out a sea of blue and white banners moving along the road and, beneath the leading one, the oak box containing signatures for Parliament.

I ran across to the metal shed.

"Father, the Jarrow marchers are coming."

"Then you'd best get that broth of yours boiling, Connie. There'll be thirty hungry men kipping down in the metal workshop tonight."

"It's just to warm up, Father. Carrots, leeks, celery and turnips from the market. Like you said."

But it wasn't the kettle drums and banners, nor the thud of feet, that was warming me up.

It was the thought of seeing Alfie Walker in his cloth cap and waistcoat, bright blue eyes peering out from a thin face.

It had all started three weeks since on a damp September morning, when a rattletrap bus drove into the yard of Father's works.

It was loaded with saucepans, piles of canvas groundsheets and copper jugs.

The driver jumped out, followed by four men. They looked thin and gaunt, as if starved of good food. Beneath their shiny dark suits they wore open-necked collarless shirts.

A young man, mid-twenties, with short brown hair and strong workman's hands, stepped forward and politely touched his cap.

"We're from Jarrow, miss. The advance guard arranging overnight stops for the marchers."

We'd heard of the plans on the wireless and how the town was dirty and rundown, the shipyards closed and the men desperate for a decent wage to feed their families.

"You'd best speak to my father. He's in the metal workshed. I'll take you across."

He was making adjustments to some soldering irons.

130

Illustration by David McAllister.

"There's some men come all the way from Jarrow, Father. Wanting lodgings next fortnight for the marchers."

The young man put out his hand.

"Alfie Walker, sir. You'll have heard of us Jarrow marchers, doubtless. I'll be blunt. Can you help us with sleeping quarters?"

Father looked the men up and down, a long, hard look that missed nothing.

"Things are tough up your way from all accounts. I'll settle for thirty. They'll have to kip down rough on the shed floor. And no fighting or drinking, mind. That's my terms."

"There'll be none of that, sir. The minister's made us take an oath against the wine of violence." The other men nodded assent.

Father threw a piece of waste metal into the bin.

"You're half skeletons the lot of you. Can you rustle up some food, Connie?"

"Corned-beef stew, and I've some bread coming out of the oven shortly."

131

The men didn't have to speak their gratitude. We could see it in their eyes.

"It's our wives and little ones we're doing it for," an older man said quietly.

"I've been a working man all my life, and I'd do just the same," Father said. "Walk every cursed mile from here to London if my girl was in need."

It was two thick slices of ham that first made me realise what a special man Alfie was.

The men had wolfed down their supper and tucked into a shoulder of ham. They were leaning against the bus, smoking pipes and yarning.

I came round the shed corner and there was Alfie, carefully stuffing his rounds of ham into a brown envelope. He flushed red when he caught me looking.

"Whatever are you doing?" I asked, flabbergasted.

He stared at the floor, mumbling an answer.

"My sister and her husband have two little bairns in Jarrow. They've not had meat in two months."

"So you're sending them yours?" I swallowed to hold back my emotions.

"It'll be a treat," he said, and I thought of the rumbling hunger in his own belly and his pinched face.

"Tell me," I said gently. "What's it like, life in Jarrow?"

"Since Palmer's shipyard shut down? No jobs, no food, no money for rent and children crying from hunger. I'm one of the lucky ones. There's only myself to look after."

"Are you a shipyard worker?"

"I was a welder. One of the lads who kept the ship from falling apart in mid-ocean." It was the first time I saw him smile.

I watched him rub tobacco in his hands and roll a cigarette.

"I'm so sorry," I said. "It's not the way things should be."

It was gone eleven when I took my leave.

"Your father's a good man, Connie. Opening his works for us men."

"Father's had it hard himself. Working the mines as a twelve-year-old lad. Then going into scrap metal and slowly climbing up the ladder."

I paused, trying to keep the emotion from my voice.

"Will I see you again?"

"I'll be back with the marchers. Back here to Barnsley. I've found a kindness here I didn't expect."

✳   ✳   ✳   ✳

How slowly those two weeks passed! Once or twice, Father eyed me.

"The Jarrow marchers will be here soon." But I wasn't biting.

My thoughts about Alfie Walker were confused and I needed space to think.

Then, at last, came the sound of kettle drums, the music of mouth organs and the tramp of boots.

I took a broom and dustpan and started busily to sweep the pavement, not wanting Alfie to know how much I'd been longing for this day.

Row after row of marching men went past, the groups splitting and wheeling away towards their various lodgings.

On the pavement, folks stood clapping and shouting out their support. Near the back of the procession was the contingent who were to stay in the metal workshop.

I scanned their faces eagerly. But Alfie Walker was not there.

Once or twice that afternoon I thought of going across and asking the men if they'd seen him. But my pride wouldn't allow it.

I was glad that father was too busy to call into the house. I didn't want him to see my disappointment.

Dusk was falling and I was about to close the shutters when I peered through the window. A solitary figure was limping along the road. I ran outside and the man's face lit up.

"Connie! I said I'd be back and here I am."

"What happened, Alfie? I thought you weren't coming."

"A bit of trouble with my boots, that's all. I didn't want to hold up the march, so I slipped behind a wall till they'd gone by."

He looked so exhausted that I spoke without thinking.

"You'd better come into the kitchen and get your socks dried out."

He looked doubtful.

"But your father . . ."

I didn't let him finish. I'd deal with Father when the time came.

"No arguments, now. It's a long, long way down to London."

He wrestled off his boots and socks and I drew in my breath. He had blisters as big as tuppennies, one looking red and raw.

"You get those feet washed under the tap in the yard."

I threw him a towel.

"Then it's iodine and plasters for you, my lad."

I'd just finished dosing him with the antiseptic on a ball of cotton-wool when Father walked in. I was expecting fireworks.

Not a bit of it.

Father stared at Alfie's blistered toes then at the bottle in my hand. Without a word, he went out to the metal shed.

Five minutes later, he returned with half-a-dozen pairs of workmen's boots. He dropped them on the floor.

"Find a pair that fits you, lad, and keep them. They'll take you to London and back easy. Drop molten tin on them and they'd laugh."

I wasn't only touched by Father's kindness. It was his tact in not asking.

We both knew full well why Alfie had set out with a pair of boots that didn't fit. He was thinking of his sister and those two young bairns.

"That's very generous of you, sir."

Father put on his grumpy voice to hide his awkwardness.

"If the tables were turned, I'd expect you to do the same for me."

People sometimes said that Father was a hard man. They were wrong. Beneath his forthright manner there was a hidden gentleness.

I thought of the countless times when he'd got in from work tired out, sat me on his lap and read me a favourite story whilst I scrabbled for the sweeties I knew he had, hidden in his pocket ready for me.

✳   ✳   ✳   ✳

Dabbing iodine on raw blisters seems a funny way to draw two people together. But it worked for us. Any awkwardness we felt soon melted away.

"It was the launches I liked best, Connie. We'd be working on a ship all winter. Then the day would come when the last rivets were fired home, the painters would put their brushes away and she would be on her way."

I nodded.

"I've seen pictures of them sliding down the slipway, royalty giving a speech and smashing a champagne bottle against the side."

He laughed out loud and the lines disappeared from his face.

"I felt that proud, thinking of all the rivets I'd fastened and how she wouldn't be afloat without my work."

I tried to imagine Alfie in a boiler suit in the dockyard as the skeleton of a great ship gradually grew around him, rivet gun in his hand.

"You must hanker after the work."

"It's like a part of me is missing."

He had to go, then, for the men were holding a meeting.

"So tomorrow it'll be off to Sheffield in the bus?" I asked casually, although I knew how much I was going to miss him.

Then he said something that jolted my whole world.

"When I told you about the shipbuilding leaving a gap, it was true."

He took my hand in his, the skin warm and rough.

"That gap's beginning to fill, Connie. You're someone very special."

"Have a good meeting and sleep well." It sounded trite, but I was so moved that I did not know what else to say.

That night, I couldn't sleep for thinking about Alfie and our blossoming

Autumn Glade

T HE golden gleams of sunlight
Enhance the autumn glade,
A place of silent wonder
The hand of God has made.

Through dewy mist of morning
The birds to sunshine fly,
To sing in shimmering distance
Amid the blue of sky.

134

relationship — however, our love was to be tested to the limit.

IT was gone ten and I was just putting out the bins for the dustcart in the morning. A pair of ginger toms were yowling hideously.

Then came the blast of whistles and the thump of heavy boots. Round the corner hurtled three of the Jarrow men, waistcoats flapping, cloth caps askew.

Behind were a squad of police constables with drawn truncheons.

Two men flew past our alleyway and then came the third. To my horror it was Alfie, red-faced and gasping for breath.

"Alfie," I hissed, clutching at his sleeve and dragging him into the alleyway. "Into the kitchen, quick!"

Seconds later a constable pulled up with a jerk.

"There was a man ran into the alleyway, miss. Did you see which way he went?"

I didn't tell the truth, but I'm not ashamed of it. Until I'd heard the story from Alfie's own lips, I was going to give him the benefit of the doubt. I pointed to the row of miners' cottages in Crosshatch Street.

"Up there, I think." I waited till the rattle of his boots had died away and went inside.

He was standing by the fire, pale and shocked.

"What happened, Alfie?"

Dennis Hardley

The leaves of gold and russet
Are falling through the air,
Afloat in breaths of autumn,
A gilding passing fair.

One feels, though winter's nearing,
With bitter wind and rain,
The sunlight only wavers —
Then spring will bloom again.

— Margaret Comer.

"A couple of local men stirred up trouble. One accused us of robbing his wife of her purse."

There was a heavy tread on the stairs and Father stood there in trousers and singlet, tough-faced.

"And did you?" The question filled the kitchen, hard, abrupt.

I don't know if Father expected a sheepish explanation or a whining excuse. He certainly didn't get it. Alfie drew himself up and I could see his fists bunching, muscles tensed.

"No, I did not, Mr Grimstone. And if you think I'm a common thief, I'll leave now."

He turned and reached for the door, but Father beat him to it.

"All right, all right. Settle down, son. My daughter's very precious to me and I needed to be sure. I believe you."

"She's precious to me, too, sir. There's no way I'd shame her."

135

I could see his eyes lingering on my dark, curly hair and bare arms poking out from the sleeves of the housecoat.

"That's all I needed to hear," Father said quietly and he rested his arm on Alfie's shoulders.

Afterwards he poured out two glasses of whisky, and I knew that the confrontation between them had established a bond. Both were blunt, honest men and they respected each other for it.

The next day, I waved goodbye to the men and watched them march off. Listening to the haunting sound of the mouth organs and kettle drums fade into the distance made London seem a billion miles away.

There'd be other girls on the way, tending to raw blisters, dishing out food and offering comfort.

"Don't bank on anything, Connie." Father's voice was unusually tender. "Nothing's certain in these difficult times."

I frowned, but deep down, I knew that he was right.

Thirteen days later, we heard the news on the wireless. The Jarrow marchers had reached London, and Prime Minister Stanley Baldwin had spurned them.

He sent out a curt message.

"I am too busy."

I slipped away to my room, my eyes damp. It seemed so cruel and heartless. I knew now I would never see Alfie again. The people of Leeds had bought tickets for the men and they were returning to Jarrow by train.

THE skies were heavy and dark and the rain was pouring down when somebody knocked on the kitchen door. The handsome young man was soaked to the skin and his eyes were black with exhaustion.

"Alfie!" I cried. "I thought —"

"I thumbed a lift in a lorry. That's why I smell of fish."

There was something in his words that made me thrown my arms open to cuddle him. But he drew back.

"I've come to say goodbye, Connie. I've nothing to offer you. No job. No money. No security."

He shook his head.

I pulled him forward, holding him like a child.

"Alfie, I'm so sorry. About the petition failing and the march. I don't know what to say . . ."

"But I do." Father was standing foursquare in the yard, head peering through the open kitchen door. "What's all this about saying goodbye?"

"I'd be a liability to her, sir. Not able to keep her as a man should."

"You young lads. You go at things like a bull at a gate. First of all, do you want to court my Connie?"

"Mr Grimstone, every step of those two hundred and eighty miles, every one of those twenty-two overnight stops, I was thinking of her. That's what kept me marching."

He managed a faint smile.

"That and your boots."

You can imagine how I flushed. What woman could hear words like that and not feel something in her heart? But Father hadn't finished.

"You say you're a welder?"

"Aye, that's my trade."

"So you know metal. How to bend and shape it. How to weld and solder."

"Since I was apprenticed twelve years ago."

"I'll give you a month's trial. If you're no good, you're out on your backside. What do you say?"

For a full thirty seconds he couldn't say anything.

"You're offering me a job?" he at last managed.

"I am that, son. If you're thinking of courting my daughter you'll need a few shillings in your pocket." He thumped Alfie on the back.

"She's got expensive tastes, has my Connie."

Father turned to me.

"And what about you, Connie, love? You haven't put your spoke in yet."

"Father." I buried my head in his greasy, metal-smelling overalls. "You're a tough old so-and-so, but I love you dearly."

My last memory before Alfie's arms circled me, his lips touching mine, was of Father stomping up the stairs in his hobnailed boots.

The moon was a yellow disc shining out amongst the scudding midnight clouds when Alfie at last went to his groundsheet bed in the metal works' shed.

✳   ✳   ✳   ✳

A year has slipped by, and it's a different world. Alfie's sister and her man have moved to Middlesbrough. He's found a job in the steel industry and takes home a healthy wage packet each week.

Alfie has taken up residence in the foreman's house behind the metalworks and I'll be joining him in three months, for our marriage plans are well laid.

And Father? As grumpy and generous as ever.

He's made no secret of our wedding present. It's to be a partnership in the metal works for Alfie.

What about those ill-fitting, battered, blister-making boots that footslogged all the way from Jarrow down through Chester-le-Street, Pity Me, Framwellgate Moor and Ferryhill on to Barnsley? They're tucked away beside Alfie's bed.

"I treasure those size sevens, Connie, my love. Them it was that brought us together." ∎

FOR me? Goodness, I'm not an invalid!" Sally laughed as I placed the luscious bunch of grapes on her bedside locker. "I feel a fraud, stranded here like a beached whale." A frown shadowed her pretty face. "What's up, Chrissie? You look a bit down in the mouth. Family OK?"

I flashed a huge grin like the Cheshire Cat.

"Yes, everyone's fine. I had an airmail from Jason this morning and Rosie's driving me up the wall, as usual!"

"Have you been clashing swords with your mum again?" she enquired, reading me like a book. Twenty-odd years ago, on our very first day at infant school, Sally and I had swapped sandals — for reasons long forgotten — and we've been standing in each other's shoes ever since, so to speak.

I hesitated.

"Well, we did have a few words yesterday. About Rosie's bedtime. She says I'm keeping the poor child up too late.

Mum's Special

by Marian Farquharson.

Seven o'clock isn't exactly midnight, is it?"

Just lately, with my husband, Jason, away for long spells serving in the Merchant Navy, I was growing a tad weary of my mother's ceaseless flow of advice — and criticism.

"She seems to forget I'm a grown woman and capable of running my own ship."

"But you'll always be her little girl, and she's only trying to help you," Sally, the peacemaker, soothed. "Everyone knows that toddlers are a handful. Talking of ships, when's your better half expected home?"

I shrugged.

"Who knows? Apparently the ship's held up with engine trouble — something highly technical. He reckons it'll be another week before they leave Buenos Aires."

"Time soon passes," she said encouragingly, "except when you're awaiting the Big Event!"

Along bustled a nurse with a slight frown and a tray of medication. Hastily gathering up my things, I blew a kiss to Sally.

"Come again soon," she begged, giving a thumbs-up sign. Always a fighter, she was putting on a brave face. With her first baby due in a few weeks' time, unforeseen problems had developed, leading to her recent admission to hospital for round-the-clock observation.

✳   ✳   ✳   ✳

I was still thinking about my oldest and dearest friend as I pushed open Mum's creaking gate. Where had all the years gone, I wondered? Only yesterday Sally and I were racing each other home from school, satchels and ponytails flying. Now Jason and I were the parents of a lively three-year-old, and Sally and Daniel could only hope and pray that their long-awaited baby arrived safely.

I tried the back door. Locked! Mum, who'd kindly offered to look after her little granddaughter on her day off whilst I visited the hospital, had probably taken her to the park to feed the ducks.

Letting myself into my old home, I settled down to wait. The grandfather clock in the parlour, five minutes fast as always, quietly ticked the seconds away.

Magic

ion by Mark Viney.

Where on earth had they got to? Four o'clock; quarter-past; and daylight beginning to fade. My concern grew. Supposing Rosie had fallen off the swings — or into the murky waters of the lake?

Thankfully, my anxious vigil at the window soon ended. I breathed a sigh of relief as I spotted them coming down the street, Rosie skipping alongside her empty buggy. She often prefers to walk on her own two feet. I rushed to open the door.

"You've not been here long, I hope?" Mum smiled, smoothing her windswept greying hair. "We'd have been back ages since, only —"

I cut her short.

"Rosie! Just look at you! Is that chocolate all down your new anorak?"

"Sorry, love, I can explain." Dabbing ineffectually at the tell-tale stains with a damp cloth, my mother went off on a tangent. "Pop the kettle on, there's a dear. I'm dying for a cuppa. You'll stay for your supper, won't you?"

"Thanks, but we'd better be on our way," I said firmly. "We don't want to hit the rush hour and I've loads to do. There's a mountain of ironing waiting . . ." What with worrying about Sally and disappointment over Jason's delayed homecoming after months at sea, the chocolate seemed the final straw! Mum had obviously been plying Rosie with the stuff, though she knows that we dole out sweeties sparingly, if at all!

Her face fell as I bundled my wriggling and protesting daughter into the buggy. I was in danger of speaking my mind and I didn't want a row in front of Rosie.

"Are you cross wiv Grandma?" Rosie asked as we joined a small queue at the bus stop.

"Cross? Goodness, no, pet." I deftly folded the buggy as the bus came round the corner. "Now, what do you fancy for your supper when we get home?"

Pursing her little rosebud mouth, she gave it serious thought.

"Choccy?" she suggested hopefully.

NEXT day we were walking back from the Humpty Dumpty Club where I work mornings as a childcare assistant. I get to take Rosie along with me, which is a big bonus — she loves running wild with the other children!

On the way home we called at Mr Green's, the appropriately named greengrocer.

"Look, Mummy!" Rosie was staring entranced at a mound of golden pumpkins, the first she'd ever seen. These were real beauties, huge round globes like miniature suns.

Well aware it would soon be Hallowe'en, with Bonfire Night to follow, she'd been pestering the life out of me for a witch's hat and fireworks!

"'I want' doesn't get!" I'd told her firmly, determined to nip pester-power in the bud — whilst investing in a few sparklers from the newsagent's when she wasn't looking.

"Those are pumpkins," I told her. "When I was a little girl Grandma used to make me a turnip lantern every year, but pumpkins are easier. You slice off the top and hollow out the shell, then you carve a funny face — and place a lighted candle inside."

Stretching out a chubby hand, she stroked the biggest one, with old Mr Green chuckling to himself in the background.

"I want pumkin!" Rosie wheedled.

"Pumpkin," I corrected, followed by, "'I want' doesn't get!" But all at once, bright and clear, half-forgotten memories came flooding back. Watching my mother make the magic lantern . . . the thrill of seeing it glowing eerily in the dark.

"We'll put it in the kitchen window, shall we? To guide folk who've lost their way," she'd say with her merry laugh, and I'd be eagerly waiting for a band of exotic travellers to come knocking at our door for shelter.

Gazing wistfully at the pumpkins, Rosie made a heartfelt appeal.

"Buy me one, Mummy! To make a funny face. Please!"

Mr Green, whose jolly red face and bushy white beard always remind me of Santa Claus, gave a knowing wink.

"Well, now, it just so happens that I'm holding a pumpkin sale today. They're all half price!"

"Oh, Mr Green." I laughed. "You know I can't resist a bargain!"

✳   ✳   ✳   ✳

Pushing the buggy down the street, with Rosie cradling a large orange pumpkin on her lap, my thoughts drifted down the years to my childhood. Things couldn't have been easy for my widowed mother, left alone with a small child. I can barely recall the handsome, cheery young man who was my father.

She'd juggled a succession of low-paid jobs with running our little house on a shoestring. But, looking back, I'd never gone short of the things that really matter, like love and laughter.

With her tremendous sense of fun, Mum was always full of bright ideas . . . letting Sally and me play gypsies on our pocket-handkerchief lawn — a travelling rug thrown over a clothes horse makes a smashing tent! — and catering for dolls' picnics with jam sandwiches and jellies made in egg cups.

But one of the biggest thrills of all had been the fairytale lantern to celebrate Hallowe'en . . . I had loved that.

And then, in a flash, I began to see things from Mum's point of view. She was still fighting my corner today, doing her utmost to help me, just as she'd always done. Once upon a time she'd worked her fingers to the bone to provide for me. Now all she could do was pass on the benefits of her long experience and I'd stubbornly chosen not to listen, resenting any criticism. What a puffed-up, self-important little madam I'd become!

Suddenly, a great wave of tender love swept over me. I thought of all those lonely years without her beloved husband by her side. I recalled the unfailing gaiety and cheerfulness that bravely hid a grieving heart . . . and I longed to run and fling my arms around her to show that I still cared.

"Rosie, love, I've just had an idea," I said as she staggered into the house, tightly clutching the precious pumpkin. "When we've made our lantern, shall we take it to show Grandma? We can put it in her window, all lit up, to welcome her home from work."

"And can I light the cangle?" she begged.

✳   ✳   ✳   ✳

Making the lantern was a team effort. I was in charge of the vegetable knife, whilst Rosie, perched aloft on the kitchen table, issued precise instructions.

"Make him look like he's laughing, Mummy! Like this — ho, ho, ho!" And she gave a loud throaty chuckle.

Carefully, I hollowed out the shell and carved merry little eyes, a triangle for a nose and a huge toothy grin.

"There we are!" I stood back to admire our joint handiwork. "He's a nice jolly chap, isn't he?"

Rosie was eyeing the chunks of golden flesh I'd carefully set aside for soup.

"Poor Mr Pumpkin, he's all chopped up." She sighed. "But he's still laughing, isn't he?"

"So he is," I agreed. "Now — I'll try to remember Grandma's soup recipe. We'll need carrots and potatoes. A nice big onion —"

"And Mr Pumpkin's inside!" she added ghoulishly.

DAYLIGHT was fading fast as we let ourselves into the empty house at the other side of town, creeping about in the gloom like conspirators. My mother works varied hours as a carer in a nearby residential home for the elderly and would be home any minute.

"We'll have to work fast," I told Rosie. Eagerly she helped me clear the window ledge — Mum loves little knick-knacks — to make a space for Mr Pumpkin. We placed him in position and carefully lit the candle. A glowing beacon to welcome her home.

Soon we heard familiar footsteps crunching on the gravel. I flung the door wide with Rosie at my side.

"Hi, Mum! It's only us. Do you like the lantern?"

Her face was a picture.

"I've not seen one in years — what a beauty! And you've made it? Aren't you clever girls!"

"Yes, Grandma," Rosie agreed proudly.

WE took little persuading to stay for supper. Mum commenced her preparations whilst Rosie whispered secrets to Mr Pumpkin and I laid the table. Suddenly she spoke.

"You seem more yourself today, Chrissie. You were a bit edgy yesterday." She gave me a searching look. "Let's be honest, dear, we've not been getting on too well lately, have we?"

Immediately I was full of remorse. Had my frustration shown so clearly?

"I'm sorry, Mum," I faltered. "It's all my fault, you know I can be tetchy."

She smiled.

"I think it's time we cleared the air, don't you? Yesterday, when you marched off in a huff, I sat and had a good old weep, remembering those happy times we used to have, wishing I could turn back the clock.

"The trouble is, dear, sometimes I forget that you're not my wee bairn any more. You're a wife and mother yourself now and I've been fussy old Mother Hen, treating you like a helpless chick. I must try to stop . . ." She was eating her heart out and I simply couldn't bear it.

"Don't, Mum," I whispered, slipping my arms around her thin shoulders, hugging her tight. "Maybe we've both misunderstood each other, but you're the best mum in the whole wide world. You're always there for me, and I know I don't deserve you. I've been so ungrateful." I fondly kissed her cheek.

"What are you and Grandma doing?" an inquisitive small voice enquired.

"We're just having a wee cuddle, love," Mum answered huskily, stretching out her hand to include Rosie. So there we stood, three generations of our small family, hugging and kissing each other as though we'd just won the Lottery. But this was one of those magic moments that money couldn't buy.

When we'd all calmed down a bit, my mother enquired about Sally.

"No news today," I told her. "This awful waiting just drags on and on and I must admit I'm worried sick."

Her face clouded.

"Poor lassie, she's not having an easy time of it. Seems only yesterday the two of you were pushing your dolly prams . . ." She gave a little sigh. "I've almost finished that pram set I'm knitting for her, so let's hope there'll very soon be a bonnie bairn wearing it."

Then she swiftly changed the subject.

"I never got a chance to explain why Rosie came back from our little outing yesterday all smothered in chocolate. Now, who should be sitting on those benches near the swings but Miss Mackay, my old housecraft teacher. You remember her? She often used to give you something for your money-box when you were a wee girl."

I nodded, remembering.

"Yes, of course I do. Didn't she retire to the Hebrides to live with her sisters umpteen years ago?" Vaguely I recalled a small dumpy figure always dressed in black, not unlike Queen Victoria. "Goodness, she must be a hundred!"

Mum snorted.

"Not quite — my schooldays are still within living memory! Anyway, she's spending a few days with a nephew and his wife who live near the park. He's something to do with computers. 'The Brainbox' she calls him . . ."

Apparently Miss Mackay had been very taken with Rosie, rewarding her good behaviour with a packet of chocolate buttons.

"She's my idea of a fairy godmother, bestowing gifts on everyone, and I simply hadn't the heart to spoil her pleasure," Mum continued fondly. "I've a strong suspicion she carries a stock of sweeties in her handbag to give to any child she meets — and probably a few biscuits for stray dogs as well!"

At that moment, the phone rang in the hall.

"See who it is, will you, love?" She was busily stirring a pan of her famous home-made soup on the stove. It smelled delicious. "I'll just keep an eye on this."

THE caller was Sally's husband, now on Cloud Nine.

"Is that you, Chrissie? Daniel here. I'm ringing to tell you we've got a wee son! He arrived this morning, safe and sound. Six and a half pounds." His normally steady voice was jerky with emotion. "They rushed Sally down to theatre around lunchtime, all safely over in half an hour . . ." Having tried my home number a few times without success, he'd guessed I might be at my mother's.

"Sally can't wait to show off the precious bundle," he went on. "The poor laddie is still nameless — we can't decide between Rory, James and Alastair, so he might get all three!"

At last I found my voice.

"Oh, Daniel, I'm so thrilled for you all! When can I see the son and heir?"

"I reckon tomorrow should be OK," he suggested. "They're quite strict about visitors, but your personal charm should get you through the roadblocks . . ."

I returned to the kitchen, walking on air.

"You'd better get knitting," I told Mum as I blinked back tears of joy. "Sally's baby arrived safely this morning — a boy — six and a half pounds, and they're both doing well."

Hovering at my side, Rosie was all ears.

"Auntie Sally's been to fetch the new baby," I told her. "You'll have a nice

Monnow Bridge, Monmouth, Wales

*I*T was so lovely to see Monmouth's river bridge with its gate tower, dating from the thirteenth century. I grew up near this ancient Welsh market town, which was formerly a border garrison between the English and the Welsh. Soldiers have been involved in the town's history for hundreds of years, and the regimental museum is well worth a visit.

Not everyone knows that Monmouth Castle was the birthplace of Henry V, who would grow up to become famous for his victory at Agincourt.

— *Mrs H.D., Stockport.*

J. CAMPBELL KERR.

new playmate when he's bigger."

"Can I feed him wiv a bottle?" she asked eagerly.

Tenderly I ruffled her tawny curls.

"We'll have to ask his mummy, pet, but I'm sure you can help push his pram."

"Now where did I put my knitting bag?" Mum was beginning a feverish search.

*   *   *   *

"Just look!" I whispered to Mum next morning. Over by the window, wielding a spoon and an empty bowl, Rosie was pretending to feed Mr Pumpkin. Mothers and babies is one of her favourite games.

"Come on, now, eat it all up," she was urging in a passable imitation of my voice. "Porridge makes you big and strong!"

"Little monkey, that's exactly what I say to her each morning — and no doubt she'll go on saying it when she's a mother herself one day," I reflected. "I suppose we're all links in an endless chain of mums."

Mum smiled.

"Nicely put, Chrissie. And we can all be very irritating, telling our offspring how to run their lives, even when they're fully grown and no longer need our good advice —" she gave me a quizzical look "— but that chain is very strong . . ."

"Unbreakable," I replied, giving her hand a little squeeze. We'd reached a perfect understanding and from now on nothing would come between us. Suddenly I knew that a mother's interference was just another word for love . . .

She wanted us to stay overnight, but tomorrow I was on early duty at the Humpty Dumpty Club.

"Can you come over to see us on Saturday and stay for supper?" I invited as we gathered up our things. "I'm going to have a bash at making pumpkin soup with the remains of Mr P. I only hope it's as good as yours — if I get stuck I'll ring you for a few tips!"

Still discussing soup recipes, we walked down the path. A great surge of happiness flooded over me. My mother and I were best friends again, Sally's precious baby was safely here, and my darling Jason would soon be home. From his perch in the kitchen window, Mr Pumpkin shed a rosy glow.

"Remember to blow out his candle before you go to bed," I reminded Mum. "You don't want to be eating blackened pumpkin skin for breakfast."

"I'll not forget," she assured me, "but I'm going to enjoy my magic lantern for a while. It's brought back a lot of happy memories."

Rosie touched my arm.

"Is he really magic, Mummy?" she whispered, eyes shining. "Can he do tricks?"

I smiled.

"Perhaps, darling. You never know . . ." ■

Step Back In Time

BORN on February 12, 1809, to Robert Darwin, a wealthy doctor, and his wife, Susannah, Charles Darwin joined a family held in high esteem.

Robert was the son of Erasmus Darwin — a renowned physicist, philosopher, inventor and poet — and Susannah, the daughter of the famous potter Josiah Wedgewood.

Charles began his scientific career aged fourteen, helping his father treat the poor of Shropshire. In the autumn of that year, 1825, he began studying medicine in Edinburgh. However, he found the reality of surgery too brutal and began to neglect his studies.

Instead, he learned taxidermy from John Edmonstone, a freed black slave, who told Charles tales of the vast South American rainforests that excited and interested him.

Much to his father's disappointment, Charles continued to sate his interest in natural history.

Concerned that this was hampering his progress in becoming a successful doctor, Robert withdrew Charles from Edinburgh and sent him to Christ's College, Cambridge, in the hope that he would become a clergyman.

But, instead of studying, Darwin chose to develop other interests including riding, shooting and a relatively new craze of collecting insects.

He began a natural history course and was recommended by his course leader to embark on an expedition to South America on *HMS Beagle.*

Although the voyage was only intended to be for two years, the survey actually took five to conduct. During this time, Charles collected hundreds of samples which he sent back to Cambridge with notes detailing his findings. These notes would showcase his abilities in theorising and also form the basis for his future work as well as establish his reputation as a learned naturalist.

By the time he returned home, he was famous in student circles as his ex-tutor had made Charles's papers available to his pupils.

By now he was well enough renowned to devote his life to science and had full support from everyone — even his father.

Charles Darwin

PA.

He continued with his research and went on to publish works such as "On The Origins Of Species" and "The Descent Of Man".

He died, after a long history of poor health, on April 19, 1882. Despite his wishes to be buried near his family home, his contemporaries demanded a state burial, and so he is interred at Westminster Abbey. ∎

BILL woke early, as he always did. All his working life he'd been awake at six o'clock and years in retirement had not changed his habits. On the bed beside him, Monty, Phyllis's elderly tabby cat, yawned and stretched. Bill scratched the cat between its ears and ran his hand down the broad, tiger-striped back.

He swung his legs out of bed and found his slippers. Making tea was another lifelong ritual. Phyllis used to say she was the luckiest woman alive to have such a thoughtful husband.

Bill drew back the curtains and inspected the weather outside. It was still dark, but the sky was clear, with no sign of rain. That was good. A drop of rain wouldn't have put him off, but a dry day with a bit of sun was a bonus. He shuffled into the kitchen and switched on the kettle. Monty wound round his legs, purring, begging for food. As a compromise, Bill put a drop of milk into the cat's saucer.

Bill still found it hard to remember he only needed the one tea cup now that Phyllis was gone. It had been eight months since she'd died and he still missed her dreadfully. There was an empty space in his life that left him drifting like a rudderless boat on a vast ocean of loss. However, he made sure nobody saw his pain. A stiff upper lip was called for; that was the way of his generation.

You've had a good life, he told himself. Now get on with whatever there is left of it. He coped by keeping the little bungalow scrupulously neat and tidy. Phyll would be so upset if he let himself go. And so, every day, he mopped the kitchen floor, polished the old-fashioned furniture they'd bought after the war and tidied Phyllis's garden. He knew his children were proud of him.

"You're doing just fine, Dad," Paul would say. "But let us know if you need anything, won't you?"

Bill said that yes, he would, but he didn't want to bother either Paul or Janet when they had such busy lives of their own.

It had been the war that had brought Bill and Phyllis together. Bill was working full-time on his parents' farm, and there had been no need for him to join up.

Illustration by Len Thurston.

148

Illustration
by Melvyn
Warren-Smith.

Lone Soldier

by Georgie Foord.

"Farming's a reserved occupation," his mother had said. "You're needed here to provide food for the people, Billy — you don't have to go and fight."

But Bill had been desperate to do his bit. He had two younger brothers to help out on the farm so, on his twenty-first birthday, he'd gone along with his two best pals, Charlie Blake and Dennis Haskell, to the recruitment centre.

As his family had waved him off at the station, his mother had shed a few tears, and his normally undemonstrative father had surprised him with a huge bear hug.

"God keep you, boy," he'd said gruffly. "I'm proud of you, you know. Go and do what you have to do and then come back safe to your mother and me."

CHARLIE, Bill and Dennis breezed through Basic Training. It all seemed like a big adventure to them. They loved the camaraderie and even the square-bashing had its moments. They all grumbled about the Drill Sergeant, of course, but privately Bill admired the way he managed to mould a bunch of raw recruits into something resembling a fighting force in just a few weeks.

Basic training led to deployment to their separate units. By a stroke of luck, Bill and Dennis found themselves on the same list, but Charlie was sent up country to somewhere in Yorkshire.

Bill was given three days' leave before being posted to France. As he walked down the lane, he passed fields belonging to the neighbouring farm. He paused, leaning on the gate to take in the peaceful scene. A lone tractor was trundling up and down the length of the field, ploughing in the stubble left behind after harvest. The tractor reached the furthest hedge, turned neatly and chugged back towards him.

Bill saw that the driver was a young woman dressed in the breeches and fawn-coloured shirt of the Land Army. The sleeves of her green sweater were knotted around her waist and he couldn't help but think she was a stunner! She stopped at the end of her furrow and ran her hand through her short, curly hair.

"Hi!" she called. "I'm Phyllis. You must be the Turners' boy from Whitegates?"

Bill grinned at her.

"That's right! News still travels fast here, I see."

She slipped the tractor into gear and waved her hand.

"Got to get on; I have to finish this lot before I stop for my dinner. See you around."

She expertly steered the tractor back on to its path and set off up the field. Bill admired the straight furrows. They were as good as any full-time ploughman's, he thought.

His mother had prepared a stupendous lunch to welcome him home. As he was sitting round the long pine table in the kitchen, with his brothers Davie and Mick, Bill felt like he'd never been away.

"I saw a young lass ploughing Dobson's barley stubble," he said as casually as he could. His mother was not deceived.

"Oh, you mean young Phyllis." She smiled. "A real livewire, that one. You'll need to be quick if you want to get anywhere with her, Billy. There's a queue of lads wanting to take her out. But it seems she's a bit choosy. There's nobody special, so I hear." She paused. "There's a dance at the hall tonight. I expect you boys will be going?"

THE village hall was heaving. Bill could hear the music from the crossroads. He recognised the fiddle and accordion of the farrier Jethro Jenkins and his nephew Duggie, who played for every event in the village.

Bill squeezed through the door and made his way round the side of the hall through the mass of khaki and blue uniforms. He made slow progress as he was greeted and slapped on the back by friends and neighbours he'd grown up with.

Out of the corner of his eye he spotted Phyllis, now wearing a simple summer dress patterned with pale yellow roses, surrounded by a trio of young men in Air Force uniforms. The "Glamour Boys", he thought crossly.

Bill made his way to the refreshment table and asked for two glasses of orange squash before casually walking over to her table.

"Hello, there!" he said. "I hoped I might see you here. Care for a drink?"

She smiled and took the cup from him. He wished fervently that he was offering champagne in the finest crystal.

"Thanks very much. It's hot in here, isn't it? Let's get some air."

Bill left the boys in blue gaping, open-mouthed, as he followed the prettiest girl he'd ever seen outside.

Bill claimed Phyllis for every dance. They jitterbugged and boogie-woogied to the uncertain rhythms of Jethro and Duggie, and he had his reward when he took her in his arms for the last waltz.

"Can I walk you home, Phyllis?"

"Well, if you don't, I don't know who will," she said, laughing.

Arm in arm they strolled down the lane in the warm summer darkness. The velvety dark sky was pierced with a million stars. To Bill, the thought that in a few days' time he would be overseas, fighting a war to preserve this idyllic way of life, was almost unbearable. They stopped at the gateway to Dobson's farm. Bill turned Phyllis to look at him.

"Be my girl, Phyllis? Will you write to me?"

She considered his request, head on one side.

"You know you're going to get a ribbing, don't you?"

Bill was confused.

"What do you mean?"

"Phyll and Bill. Bill and his Phylly. Sounds corny, doesn't it?"

He laughed.

"I see what you mean. But if you can stand it, I'll try to be brave!"

She gave him a quick kiss on the cheek.

"So that's settled then. I'm your girl, and you'd better remember it, Billy-boy."

She was as good as her word. Letters found their way to him in France. They were full of news about his family and the farm — describing the changing seasons, keeping his special corner of Dorset fresh in his mind. She sent a small photograph of herself which Bill placed carefully in his pocket book. He kept it with him, day and night.

ANY illusion Bill and Dennis had fostered about war being a glorious adventure were soon dispelled as they were faced with the reality of fighting in France. In June of 1940, the comrades-in-arms found themselves amidst the carnage on the beach at Dunkirk as the British Army tried desperately to escape. Helping the wounded, carrying stretchers for the medics, trying to stay alive — they waited for their turn to be rescued. As the

Hints Of Winter

A POOL of winter sunshine
On frost-embroidered leaves,
There's snowdust on the rooftops
On chimney pots and eaves.
A robin on the trellis
With bib of cherry red,
Watches out with beady eyes
For tiny crumbs of bread.

small boats came in, men formed orderly lines, and with shells falling around them, waded out through the surf to be taken out to the larger vessels.

Bill stumbled across a soldier with a terrible head wound. He bandaged the man as best he could, and carried him down to the surf edge to wait for the next boat. Dennis was already waiting in line in the water ahead of him and he turned to urge Bill to join him.

"Come on, man! It's our turn!"

"You go on. I'll see to this bloke first. He's in a bad way," Bill shouted back.

As he hauled the casualty on to the boat, Bill caught a stray bullet in his thigh.

Bill ignored the damage to his leg and worked tirelessly, moving the wounded down to the water's edge and helping them get away. Finally, it was his turn. He was exhausted and it was all he could do to pull himself into the boat. He collapsed in relief, as strong capable hands tied a bandage around his thigh.

He was hoisted aboard the paddle steamer that would take them back across the Channel and, by chance, found he was lying on a mattress next to the stranger he'd helped earlier. The man was barely conscious but there was something about him that stirred Bill's memory. He looked into the man's shattered face and recognised his friend, Charlie Blake.

"Charlie!" he whispered. "Charlie, it's Bill. Billy Turner. You're safe now, mate. You'll be OK. Just hang in there."

Charlie's eyes fluttered open.

"Bill!" he muttered. "Fancy seeing you here. How're you doing?"

Tears stung Bill's eyes.

"You get some kip now, mate. We'll soon be home and we'll get you fixed up."

Bill held Charlie in his arms all through the long night but, some time just towards dawn, his friend gave a gentle sigh and slipped away. Better this way, perhaps, Bill thought. He was so very badly injured. When he got home he would go and see Charlie's parents and tell them what had happened, how their son was a hero and that he didn't suffer.

The pond has frozen over,
The air is crisp and chill,
There's ice-curls forming patterns
On window-pane and sill,
The grass stands to attention,
Each blade a frosted spear,
And nature leaves her calling card
That winter's almost here.

— *Kathleen Gillum.*

BILL was sent home to recuperate from his injury, and on a sunny morning, between haymaking and harvest, he and Phyllis were married in the village church.

Bill, leaning on a stick, proudly walked his bride down the aisle. She looked a picture, he thought. His mum and Mrs Dobson had worked wonders. They had conjured up a wedding gown from a couple of damask tablecloths, with lace trimmings from some net curtains, redundant now that the blackout was in force.

The vicar's wife had raided her garden and contributed some sprigs of creamy, orange-fragrant philadelphus blossoms, which Phyllis had tucked into her dark curls. She also carried a posy of Queen Anne's lace, meadowsweet and palest pink dog roses, picked from the hedgerow that morning. The landlord at the Red Lion donated ham sandwiches and a barrel of beer; Jethro and Duggie played their hearts out; and everyone agreed it was the finest wedding you could wish for.

The train took them the few miles to Swanage where Miss McIver's boarding house provided a room on the fourth floor. Inconveniently, the bathroom was down on the first floor, but their eyrie up in the rooftops had a spectacular view of the bay.

"I'm sorry it's not the Ritz, love," Bill said apologetically.

"Who wants the stuffy old Ritz? You don't get a sea view at the Ritz, do you?"

Bill gazed at this wonderful girl who, miraculously, he could now call his wife.

"I love you, Mrs Turner, with all my heart," he said, crushing her close to

153

him. "I'll never let you down, not if I can help it."

She stirred in his arms.

"Just stay safe, Billy. No more heroics, you hear me? You'll be needed back here when all this nonsense is over."

Bill and Dennis were sent to North Africa. They'd thought fighting in France was bad enough, with the rain and the mud, but the blistering desert heat was beyond imagination. The sand got everywhere: in their food, drinking water and kitbags. Their feet swelled and sweated in the heavy boots.

They took part in the push for Tobruk. That was when Dennis dropped at Bill's side, felled by a sniper. That's it, Bill thought. Now it was just him, and he resolved to stay alive and get back home to Phyllis. He just had to follow orders and not take unnecessary risks. He had to stay safe for Phyllis.

FORTY years later, Bill joined a veterans' trip to the war cemeteries at Tobruk. He found Dennis's grave in an orderly row of identical white headstones. Bill was struck by the utter peace of the scene now, in contrast to the hell-hole he'd known. The cemetery was lovingly tended by Libyan gardeners, who carefully weeded and watered the few hardy shrubs that could survive there.

Dennis, only twenty-three when he died, had lain in this quiet place, under the endless African sky, when he should have been carving out a career, marrying his sweetheart and raising a family. Bill shed a tear for him, and for all the countless thousands of young men and women of that lost generation. Nationality didn't enter into it now, he thought. Allies and foes, they were all victims of their masters.

✳   ✳   ✳   ✳

The years struggled on towards peace. At long last Bill had been given his demob papers and he went home to start married life with Phyllis. The immediate problem was trying to find somewhere to live. Bill realised at once that there was no place for them on the farm. The land was already supporting his parents, together with Davie and his wife, as well as young Mick. Bill managed to find a couple of rooms for them to rent in the nearby town. It was just a bedroom and living-room, with a kitchenette in the hallway, and they had to share the bathroom with two other couples.

"I know it's not much, love," Bill had said. "But we'll get by, and things will get better, I promise you. As soon as I get a job, we can start saving."

Farming had been his trade. He couldn't face working indoors so he took a job with a haulage company. He travelled the length and breadth of the country in his big lorry, enjoying the freedom of the open road.

Phyllis worked as a filing clerk in an office and, between the two of them, they scrimped and saved. After a year or two they had enough put by for a deposit on a small terraced house. It was a tiny two-up, two-down, but it had a scullery with a gas cooker, and a bathroom built on at the back, and a little scrap of garden where they could sit on summer evenings. Phyllis was so proud of her house. She scrubbed and polished tirelessly. She made curtains, cushion covers and rag rugs, and turned the bleak little place into a cosy home for the two of them.

"Now," she said to Bill. "Now we can think about a family!"

Janet was born a couple of years later, and Paul came along to complete the family when Janet had just turned five and started school.

The years passed. Bill had to give up driving when the old wound in his leg started causing problems, but the company recognised a loyal worker and eventually he became Depot Manager. Janet and Paul grew up, got through their teenage years without causing their parents too many problems, and eventually married and produced grandchildren for Bill and Phyllis. Life was good to the Turner family.

However, Bill never forgot his Army pals. The Regiment, as he'd known it, was amalgamated with others into a larger force, but he was a loyal member of the Old Comrades' Association and never missed the annual reunion, or Remembrance Day parade. He enjoyed meeting up with the men he'd served with, swapping life histories and telling the "do you remember old-so-and-so?" stories.

He was aware that, each year, one or two faces were missing, but it had been a shock when the Brigadier had announced that as numbers had dwindled to just a handful, the Association was being disbanded. When the Brigadier had asked if anyone would like to parade for the final time in November, Bill had been the first to put up his hand.

BILL studied his face in the bathroom mirror. It was funny how you weren't aware of getting older, he thought, and then one day there's your grandad staring back at you. He shaved carefully, not wanting to risk a nick on his chin today. His hand was a bit shaky. It was probably a good thing that Paul had insisted he swap his old-fashioned, cut-throat razor for one of the new-fangled safety things.

He patted his face dry and fastened the top button of his thick flannel vest. He lifted his new white shirt off the hanger and slipped it over his skinny shoulders. He then fastened the gold cufflinks bearing the Regimental crest. Phyllis had given them to him for their Golden Wedding and they were among his most precious possessions. He tucked the shirt into his trousers, hooked the dangling braces over his shoulders and slipped his feet into shiny black shoes. He knotted the stripy Regiment tie; perhaps for the last time, he thought suddenly, with a pang of regret.

He opened the bureau drawer and lifted out the small leather boxes where his medals lay, the ribbons as bright as the day he'd received them. With trembling hands he pinned them to his jacket: the Africa Star with its sand-coloured ribbon, striped with red and two shades of blue; the red, white and blue War Medal, which everybody had for being there, and finally, the maroon and dark blue of the Distinguished Conduct Medal. They'd given him that one for getting the wounded lads off the beach at Dunkirk. He was a bit embarrassed about it, as he felt that anybody would have done the same, but Phyll and his mum and dad were immensely proud of him.

He flicked an invisible speck of dust off his beret and rubbed the already gleaming badge with his hanky. He carefully placed the beret on his head at exactly the right angle, then stepped back, ramrod straight, to see the full effect in the hall mirror.

The front door opened.

"Very smart, Corporal," Paul said, tucking a poppy into his father's buttonhole. "You're a credit to the Regiment!"

Young Billy followed his father into the small hallway. At fifteen, he already towered over his grandfather. Dressed in his Army Cadet uniform, he was on parade today as well. Both Paul and Bill had tried to dissuade him, but young Billy had his heart set on a career in the Army.

THE Assembly Point is crowded. A sea of men and women in military and civilian uniforms mill around trying to line up in their formations. Orders are shouted; bandsmen are tuning up. Bill looks eagerly for the comrades who'd promised to parade with him today. There was no sign of Bert or Walter, or old Teddy with his guide dog. Even Alf, who'd offered to push Clem in his wheelchair, was nowhere to be seen. Increasingly agitated, Bill stares wildly around him. Then the truth dawns: he's the only one there.

"Never mind, Dad," Paul says. "You can stand with me and we'll watch Billy doing his stuff."

Bill glares at his son.

"I've come to march today, and march I will," he says.

The order is given:

"By the left, qu-i-i-ck march!"

The band starts up and Bill falls in behind the rearmost rank and, head held high, proudly steps off on his left foot, arms swinging, on his last parade. He takes a deep breath. The cold November air hits his chest like a bullet and he gasps and falters for a moment.

Then, suddenly, he realises he's not alone. A host of shadowy figures are marching alongside him. He recognises Charlie Blake and Dennis Haskell, and there's old Clem, standing tall on his own two legs! Bill looks around and spies young Phyllis standing at the roadside with Paul, smiling and waving.

Happily, Bill falls into line with his chums and marches proudly to the beat of the drum. The spectators at the roadside see only a solitary, proud old man stepping out bravely, but Bill knows that his comrades have come to help him out on his last parade. The last soldier has rejoined the Regiment. ■

A Winter's Tale

by June Davies.

MEGAN awoke with a start. Monday morning! Wriggling around, she squinted at the bedside clock. It was only 6.45, thank goodness!

"Where's the fire?" Hugh mumbled.

"Thought I'd overslept," she whispered.

"It's the crack of dawn, love." With a sigh, Hugh drifted back into sleep.

She and Hugh had returned from honeymoon on Saturday evening, and this was her first "proper" day as Chloe and Pippa's mother. Slipping from bed, Megan checked a mental list of things she had to remember for her stepdaughters going to school. Not that there was much for her to do. The children's grandmother, Enid Warburton, had seen to that.

The big, flagged kitchen was chilly as she moved noiselessly about, glancing round at the sound of Hugh's footsteps.

Illustration by Sue Heslop.

"I wasn't expecting you up so early!" She raised her face for his kiss.

"I thought I'd do a couple of hours' work before the office opens," Hugh explained, disappearing into his study and emerging with a battered briefcase. "January is always a busy time, and after two weeks away there'll be masses to catch up with. Need a hand with anything?"

She shook her head.

"Enid's left everything just so. She's stocked up the fridge and the freezer,

157

and there's lots of fresh stuff in the pantry."

"That's Enid!" he replied fondly. "She likes nothing better than keeping busy and organising things."

"Hugh, I still feel a bit mean about Enid moving out," Megan began uneasily. "I mean, I'm glad we're alone with the girls, but even so . . ."

"It was Enid's decision," he replied, draining his coffee cup and putting on his coat. "We both tried to persuade her to stay."

Megan nodded, seeing him to the door. Beyond the garden, the beech wood that gave their old house its name was blurred by the slanting grey rain.

"I really do want to be a proper mother to Chloe and Pippa — not just your new wife."

"Of course you do, and you will be!" he answered, giving her a quick kiss and starting up the car. "Don't wait up for me, I'll probably be late."

AFTER breakfast, Chloe and Pippa did their usual round of bird and squirrel feeding in the garden, and when it was time to leave for the school bus, Megan glanced around to check nothing had been left behind. "Right, we're off!"

"Lunchboxes!" Pippa piped up. "We haven't got them!"

Megan's blood ran cold. Why hadn't she realised the girls would need lunchboxes?

"Gran said she'd leave a note," Chloe went on. "On the fridge door!"

Megan stared at the tall door with its colourful magnets, paintings and reminders. Right there in the centre was a neat, detailed note about what each girl had for lunch. How could she have missed it?

She groaned, her eyes on the clock. There'd just be enough time to cut and fill sandwiches, sort out fruit and yoghurt.

"Girls, get yourselves into the car!"

"We always walk down the lane to the bus," Chloe returned. "Gran says walking is better for us."

"She's right," Megan answered, swiftly washing tomatoes and apples. "But by the time I've done your lunches, it'll be too late for you to walk."

"We can take the short cut through the wood," Pippa suggested.

"I don't know the wood," Megan replied, buttering bread.

"But we always go by ourselves," Chloe protested. "We're not babies!"

"Lunchboxes," Megan announced, placing a box in each girl's hand and shunting them towards the front door. "Car!"

※　　※　　※　　※

Enid Warburton wandered about her cottage beside the church, brooding.

"You'll have to snap out of this, my girl!" she scolded herself.

She was vigorously clearing moss from the garden path when her neighbour popped his head over the low wall.

"How are you settling in?" Billy Clegg asked genially. "Need any help?"

"I can manage, thank you."

"Feeling lonely, I'll bet." He considered. "You should get yourself a dog. Or a cat, maybe. I'd be lost without Wolfie."

"I don't care for pets. I couldn't have one in the house."

"They're wonderful companions, Enid," he replied quietly.

Enid's expression softened.

"Sorry to bite your head off. I'm in a foul mood today!"

Billy smiled reassuringly.

"It was bound to happen," he commented sensibly. "It's been a long while since Grace passed away."

"Pippa was barely toddling!" She sighed. "And of course Hugh would want to marry again. It's just . . . I only moved out yesterday and I'm missing my girls already, Billy! Taking care of them and looking after Hugh and Gracie's house has been my whole life these past years."

Billy looked thoughtful.

"They asked you to stay on at Beechwood, didn't they? It's not too late to change your mind."

Enid shook her head.

"Two women in the same kitchen doesn't work. Besides, Megan has given up her job to stay at home."

"She'll likely need some help getting settled," Billy persisted gently. "She hasn't any family nearby, remember."

"Megan's an independent young woman with a new home and family. She won't welcome any interference."

"You won't know until you try!"

"The truth is," Enid murmured unhappily, "I just don't think I can face seeing another woman taking Gracie's place and being mother to her children!"

WITH the children at school, Megan's thoughts drifted back to the very first afternoon Hugh had brought her to Beechwood. It was early summer. A glorious day.

Chloe and Pippa were shy and quiet, staying close to their grandmother, and Enid was friendly and polite. She'd prepared a delicious lunch, which they ate in a sunny corner of the lawn.

"It's such a beautiful garden, and it's huge!" Megan had said afterwards, when she and Hugh were strolling across to where garden became flower-filled meadow before meandering away into the old beech wood. "I especially love the pond, and you've so many bird tables and nest boxes!"

"It's all the girls' doing. They love animals. Birds, squirrels, hedgehogs, rabbits . . . Chloe and Pip feed and water them all, twice a day, regular as clockwork!" he answered proudly. "Grace would've preferred a modern town house but I desperately wanted our children to grow up here, where my brother and I had such a carefree childhood."

"You lived here when you were little?"

"Apart from university, I've lived at Beechwood my whole life!" He smiled, adding seriously, "Children need space to play. Gary and I spent our childhood outdoors. We even built a hide-away in the wood where we could watch badgers and foxes. We'd camp there with our dog.

"I'm not sure who enjoyed those camping trips more, Gary and me, or old Rusty. You've never seen a dog with a bigger grin . . ." Hugh laughed, remembering. "Ear to ear, it was!"

Megan laughed with him, gazing up into his warm brown eyes.

"Do you still have a dog?"

He shook his head.

"Not since before I married. Grace was very house-proud, she wasn't fond of animals. Enid feels the same, so the girls having pets has never been an option. What about you?"

"My family have always had a dog," she replied. "But since I left home, I've lived in flats and been out at work all day, so it wouldn't be fair to have a pet."

"Something for the future, perhaps?" Hugh said, and a sudden tenderness in his eyes held the hope their futures might be shared . . .

MEGAN was busying herself in the kitchen when she spotted the girls emerging from the wood, plaits and school scarves flying.

"How was school?" Megan beamed as they shed coats and school bags in the hall. "Tea's nearly ready."

"We're not having tea now, are we?" Pippa queried, standing stock-still on the stairs. "We've got to go back to the wood!"

"We always go out before tea!" Chloe added.

"I know you do, and you still have time." Megan smiled. "Change out of your school things and away you go. But remember, you're to be back soon!"

They were downstairs again in an instant, rummaging about in the hall cupboard and clattering back and forth before running out into the garden. Megan watched them topping up the water bowls, scraping out a can of food on to the hedgehogs' stone and scattering seeds and nuts for the late birds and rabbits before they disappeared from sight towards the wood.

It was almost dusk when the doorbell rang. It was Enid.

"Enid! Won't — won't you come in?" Megan faltered, self-conscious about inviting Enid Warburton into the house that had been her home until yesterday. "Goodness, you look frozen!"

"It's bitter!" Enid agreed, following her into the warm kitchen. "My neighbour says we'll have snow before the week is out, and I think he's right."

"Would you like a cuppa?"

"Coffee, please," Enid responded, catching her breath at the sight of Megan moving about the kitchen just as Gracie had once done. "Are the girls back

Twyford Lock, Herts., England

*M*Y mother phoned me from Britain, excited to tell me to make sure I got my "Friend" that week! She remembers Twyford Lock from when she was a little girl watching the lock-keeper at work, and has described often the horse-pulled barges, laden with timber, passing through the lock on the way to the timber yards. On the way back they'd sometimes have a load of hay or straw.

Boating was also popular on the rivers, especially on warm summer evenings — which there seem to have been plenty of in her day!

— *R.S., Alberta, Canada.*

J. CAMPBELL KERR.

from school yet?"

"Been in and gone out again." Megan smiled, bringing the mugs.

"I never could keep those girls indoors," Enid remarked, sipping her coffee. "At least they're always back promptly before dark. Oh, I almost forgot —

"I was baking today," she went on, hesitantly taking a plastic box from her bag. "It's just a cherry cake . . ."

As Megan was lifting the lid, Chloe and Pippa burst into the kitchen. Megan hadn't even noticed that the rain had started again, but the girls were soaked through, rivulets of rainwater dripping from their hair and clothes.

"Gran!" they chorused, flinging themselves at her.

"You've made us a cake!" Chloe said excitedly.

"Never mind cakes!" Enid chided, gently towelling each girl's cold, wet face. "Whatever were you doing out without macs and wellies?

"Megan." She straightened up, turning to the younger woman. "You really must get them into a hot bath and dry clothes as quick —"

However, Megan was already bustling Chloe and Pippa from the room.

"Can I give you a hand?"

"No, thanks," Megan called over her shoulder. "I can manage . . ."

The kitchen was suddenly silent, save for the rattle of icy rain against the window-panes. Putting on her coat, Enid called goodbye up the stairs, slipped from the house and scurried through the rainy night down towards Church Mews.

P IPPA'S very snuffly," Megan said next morning. "I think she should stay home from school today."

"Sounds sensible. Don't look so worried, love!" Hugh said, giving her a reassuring hug. "It's just a chill. A day indoors and Pip will be as right as —"

"Please don't say rain!" She grimaced, kissing him goodbye. "I should have made sure the girls had on their macs and wellies!"

Later, when Chloe had set off for the school bus, Megan took a mug of hot blackcurrant juice up to Pippa.

"Have I got to stay in bed all day?" she grumbled. "Can't I go for a walk in the woods? I bet a walk in the woods would do me good."

"You can't go out. It's much too cold," Megan replied. "But you could get up and have a duvet day."

"What's that?" Pippa asked curiously.

"It's when you chill out in your pyjamas, snuggle up in a duvet and do whatever you want." Megan smiled.

After they had watched a video and played three games of "Haunted Castle", Megan said, "I think I'll call your gran. I didn't see her before she went home last night."

There was no reply from Enid's cottage, and Megan had just put down the phone when it started ringing. She picked it up on the first ring.

"Hello, love. Yes, we're fine . . . I see . . . we will. Bye, love."

She returned to the living-room.

"Your dad has to go to Leeds. He'll be home late."

"Again? We didn't see him before we went to sleep last night!" Pippa complained. "And we want to ask him something really important!"

"Anything I can help with?"

Pippa screwed up her face, shaking her head. Megan smiled to herself, wondering what the big secret could be.

T HE first ragged snowflakes were swirling when Chloe cannoned from the woods, across the garden and indoors. Shrugging off her coat, she at once went into an animated huddle with her younger sister.

"Hi, Chloe," Megan greeted her, popping her head around the living-room door. "If you're going outdoors again, wrap up really well. And be as quick as you can — it's already getting dusky."

"I won't be long." Chloe nodded, darting past her and upstairs to change.

Darkness was fast falling and despite her promise, Chloe had not returned. Megan found Pippa at the living-room window, staring out into the snow-blanketed garden. There was not a breath of wind now. The flakes were huge and downy, falling thick and fast. Megan fought to quell her increasing panic.

"I have to go and look for her, Pippa," she murmured. "I don't know the woods well. Can you tell me which way Chloe might have gone?"

"I know exactly where Chloe went," Pippa answered, her eyes wide and scared. "She's gone to our holly house, but I don't know why she hasn't come back! She said she'd be quick and —"

"Shhh, everything's going to be all right, Pip." Megan gathered the tearful little girl into her arms. "What's this holly house? Where is it?"

"Holly house is our secret place." Pippa sniffed, throwing off her duvet. "It's near the brook. I'll show you —"

＊　　＊　　＊　　＊

"Thanks for putting up with me this afternoon, Billy," Enid Warburton said as they trudged to her front door. "I've been miserable company."

Billy shrugged, stamping the snow from his boots before stepping into the tidy hallway and putting down the tins of gloss and parcels of wallpaper.

"Best to get out and do something."

"We've certainly done that!" she agreed, surveying the heap of purchases. "But I just can't shake off this awful emptiness! It's perfectly clear Megan doesn't need my help. Nor do my granddaughters any more."

She was interrupted by the ring of the telephone, and Billy knew from Enid's sharp questions and knotted brow that it was serious. Replacing the receiver, her troubled eyes met his.

"Will you drive me up to Beechwood? I'll explain on the way."

Megan was waiting at the doorstep, already dressed and ready to go out.

163

"Thanks for coming, Enid. Hello, Mr Clegg. Enid, will you please stay with Pippa while I look for Chloe? She's —"

"That doesn't make sense," Enid cut in firmly. "Have you ever been to the girls' holly house? I thought not. I'll go, and you stay with Pip."

"Absolutely not," Megan returned vehemently. There was no way she was about to let the elderly woman go out searching in a snowstorm!

Illustration by Neil Reed.

"Hang on, the pair of you," Billy began in his unruffled way. "Holly house, is that the hide Hugh and Gary built when they were lads?"

Enid nodded.

"It's completely overgrown with holly now. The girls have it for their playhouse and —"

"That's settled, then. Enid, get me a good strong spade." He turned to Megan. "You and I will go and fetch her while Enid holds the fort."

With Enid and Pippa watching from the window, Megan followed Billy down the garden and into the wood. She soon lost all sense of time and distance. The wood and the walking went on and on.

"There's the hide!" Billy shouted at last, ploughing knee-deep through the snow. "Chloe! Chloe!"

There was no answering shout and fear drained every ounce of strength from Megan's limbs. She watched Billy putting his shoulder to the frozen door. It groaned and gave way.

Their torch beams spilled inside, falling upon Chloe. She was huddled in the corner, her arms tightly wrapped about a small black and white bundle. Very, very slowly, the girl raised her head and opened heavy-lidded eyes.

"Megan," she mumbled through numb lips. "He's so little and cold . . ."

✳   ✳   ✳   ✳

When they were once more in the warmth and safety of the living-room, Chloe looked exhausted but none the worse for her adventure. She and Pippa were sharing the duvet, the black and white puppy cradled between them.

"He will be all right, won't he?" Pippa raised fearful eyes to Megan. "He's not going to die?"

"He's not injured, and he doesn't seem ill," Megan replied, gently smoothing her hands over the pup's scrawny body and looking into his snub face and huge, clear eyes. "We'll take him to the vet for a check-over tomorrow, but I'm sure he's going to be just fine."

"Oh, my word!" Enid exclaimed, aghast, as she came in with a tray of hot soup and stopped in her tracks. "Megan, you're surely not allowing that animal inside the house? It isn't —"

"Enid, here's the crusty bread you asked me to bring!" Billy interrupted hastily, following Enid into the room. "Shall we eat up while everything's nice and hot?"

"But —" she began sharply, biting her tongue when she caught Billy's eye. Pursing her lips, Enid said nothing more as she offered the home-made soup.

"Thanks, Enid," Megan murmured, looking up from where she was sitting cross-legged on the floor. "For everything you've done tonight. Both of you."

"That's what family is for," she replied briskly. "We were glad to help."

While they drank their soup, Billy considered the sleeping dog. "Doesn't look more than ten or twelve weeks old, does he?"

"Perhaps somebody got him for Christmas," Chloe suggested. "And got fed up with him."

"Could be. I've already phoned the police and the animal shelter, just in case anyone's looking for him and wants him back," Megan commented. "Although from all you've told us, that doesn't seem likely."

"He's still cold, Megan!" Pippa exclaimed, her fingers wrapped around the small pink pads. "Feel his paws!"

"I'll do a water bottle. As long as it's not too hot and well wrapped so he can't hurt himself." She ruffled Pippa's hair. "It'll soon warm his cold feet!"

"You stay with the girls," Enid said unexpectedly. "I'll get the hottie."

She returned with a hot-water bottle swathed in an old rug under one arm, and a large basket beneath the other.

"If you're determined to have that dog indoors, you'll need somewhere for it to sleep," she began crisply. "It can have my old laundry basket. I needed a new one anyway."

Pippa and Chloe pounced upon the treasure, immediately arranging cushions, outgrown woollens and the water bottle inside it.

"It's perfect, Gran!" they chorused.

A SHORT while later, Hugh returned from Leeds to find everyone talking and laughing in the living-room; his wife sitting on the floor and his daughters either side of a laundry basket that had a tiny, scruffy-looking black and white dog fast asleep in it.

"It's a long story, love!" Megan chuckled, padding across the room in her socks to greet him. "I'll get your supper. Hot chocolate for everyone else?"

"Not for us," Billy replied, standing up stiffly. "I've an early start tomorrow. I've been roped in to helping Enid wallpaper her front room."

Megan's face lit up.

"Oh, I love painting and decorating! Can I come and —" she asked enthusiastically, before breaking off self-consciously. "Sorry, I didn't mean to barge in like that . . ."

"It — it'd be smashing if you'd come and help," Enid ventured quietly.

"See you in the morning, then!" Megan beamed, impulsively giving the older woman a quick hug.

"That'll be nice," Enid replied, a little taken aback but not at all displeased at Megan's spontaneous gesture. "If you've time, perhaps you could help me choose some curtains?"

ENID and Billy said their goodnights and started homewards and Chloe and Pippa launched into telling their tale all over again.

"We got off the school bus yesterday afternoon and started walking home," Chloe began. "Pippa saw a car stop down the lane. The driver opened the door and threw a sack out, then he drove off again really fast."

"When we got near the sack, we could hear crying. So we untied it, and found him," Pippa added.

"We hid him in the holly house and came home," Chloe continued. "Later, we went back with some food and milk.

"After I'd fed him this afternoon, he looked so little and scared, I couldn't bear to leave him there all alone," Chloe finished, lowering her eyes. "So I stayed a bit longer. Then the snowstorm came."

Hugh shook his head.

"Chloe, it's freezing tonight! If Billy and Megan hadn't found you . . ." he began. "Why didn't you just bring him home when you found him?"

The sisters exchanged an anxious look.

"We were afraid you wouldn't let us look after him," Chloe answered at last. "We're not allowed pets."

"Even if we couldn't keep him," Megan began gently, meeting Hugh's gaze above the girls' heads, "we would've taken him in and helped him."

"Meg's right," Hugh said, his arm tightening about her slim shoulders. "But if you don't tell us things, we can't help you sort them out."

Both girls nodded.

"Dad . . . can we keep him?"

Hugh smiled.

"It's up to Meg. She'll have to take care of him while we're out all day."

The sisters turned imploring eyes to Megan and she smiled.

"On one condition. You think up a really good name for him."

Once the girls were in bed, Hugh drew Megan down beside him on the settee, kissing her as they snuggled up together in the dancing firelight.

Beyond the bay window, the snow had almost ceased. The garden was brilliant and glistening, and far away in the wood a lone owl hooted.

They kissed just as Chloe's voice drifted down from the landing.

"Can Paws come and sleep upstairs with us?"

Reluctantly, Hugh released Megan from his embrace. She laughed softly, brushing his lips with the lightest kiss before rising from the settee, extending her hand so he might follow.

"I'll carry the basket, you bring the pup!" ■

The Most Beautiful Doll In The World

by Celia Rogers.

Illustration by
Majken Thorsen.

EVERY year, on my birthday, a parcel arrived at our house. It was always for me, from my mam's friend Clara.

I hardly knew Auntie Clara. She had been my mother's bridesmaid and best friend at school, though now they met rarely. Auntie Clara had moved to London, which I knew was a long way from Lancashire.

But she always kept up her habit of sending me a special present on my birthday, because she was my godmother. She had never forgotten me once, in seven years.

This year, the creased brown paper parcel was tied up with string and had six stamps stuck on the front. My mam, always the conservationist, immediately took the parcel off me and set to work undoing the knots and folding up the brown paper and string. She handed me a big shoebox.

I cried with delight when I saw what was inside, wrapped round and round with white tissue paper. My fingers were shaking — my two sisters hung over my shoulder, breathing down my neck to try to see what I'd got.

Inside that shoebox, all wrapped up, was the most beautiful sleeping dolly I'd ever seen. She was wearing a long pale pink gown.

"Oh, how beautiful," I whispered, reaching out to this treasure.

Joanne and Gillian's faces tightened.

"It's not fair she should have a doll. We never get anything from Auntie Clara on our birthdays."

Mam told them — for the umpteenth time — that I was named Clara after Auntie Clara, and that's why I was very special to my auntie, as she had no little girls of her own. Most important of all, Auntie Clara was my godmother.

But this didn't satisfy my sisters.

"Our godmothers never send us presents like that," they moaned.

Mam only shrugged.

"I can't help that, can I? It's giving, not the gift, that counts. And you shouldn't be jealous of your sister. Perhaps if you ask Clara nicely, she'll let you look at her dolly. Maybe she'll even let you hold her, but only if you both stop pulling faces now."

Then she gave them one of her looks.

My sisters dutifully asked if they could pick her up, and I graciously agreed. We all looked over my dolly in meticulous detail. My sisters said that she was almost lifelike and thought that maybe she might speak. But, even though she didn't say a word, they agreed she was wonderful and admired her soft black eyelashes.

I particularly admired the doll's little white shoes, with a tiny button on the side to hold the strap across her feet, and her long white silk stockings. She had a full set of white underwear, too — a vest and pantaloons with lace on them. We all checked and touched the fine cotton reverently, in turn.

The three of us were smitten, and I was so glad she was mine. Her eyes were blue; her hair was dark brown and felt like feathers under my fingers.

"She's the most lifelike dolly I've ever seen," Gillian whispered.

I let each of my sisters pick her up and hold her for a few moments before I put her carefully back in her box.

MY dolly had a face of such beauty, and was so precious to me, that I used to worry whenever Joanne and Gillian wanted to play with her. They were continually at me to get her out of her shoebox, wanting to pick her up and nurse her. I was afraid they would drop her or be rough with her.

So I hid her in a secret place only I knew about, and I wouldn't tell them where it was, even when Gillian gave me a Chinese burn in the scullery. I just screeched and Mam came clattering downstairs.

"Whatever's the matter now?"

"Nothing, I fell over, that's all," I said, rubbing my arm. We sisters had a code, we never told tales on each other.

My dolly was rehoused in Mam's wooden bedding box under the stairs, well away from Joanne and Gillian. The stairs in our house were so steep that under the stairs was like a little room. I'd sit on the bedding box and play with her in there.

I named her Elizabeth after Princess Elizabeth, who was in all the newspapers. I thought the princess was almost as beautiful as my Elizabeth. Eventually, my older sisters lost interest in dollies, so Elizabeth was able to sit in state on the settee next to the fire.

I WAS glad I'd given my beautiful doll the name Elizabeth when we were invited to watch the Coronation at my Auntie Maggie's. Princess Elizabeth was about to be made Queen of Great Britain in London. I wondered if Auntie Clara would be in Westminster Abbey.

There were twelve of us, sitting straight on hard wooden chairs in Auntie Maggie's front room on Coronation Day, all looking respectful. Relations sat in the front row, Grandma and Grandad in the middle and the children on the floor. Those neighbours who had lent chairs were allowed to sit behind.

We all stared in absolute silence at the tiny twelve-inch television set as if it was a miracle — which it was, for me. Nobody moved a muscle, except for Grandma, who kept saying, "Well, I never!"

It was the first time anybody in our family had seen a television set, and Auntie Maggie was full of pride as she passed round tinned salmon sandwiches and pieces of pork pie. We all just stared transfixed at the screen, hardly noticing what we were eating.

I particularly admired the long velvet train that the new Queen wore. I wanted one for my Elizabeth. I imagined it would be red, and I loved the edges that were made of something called ermine.

"What's ermine?" I whispered to Mam.

"It's a special sort of fur," she whispered back.

"Shush," everybody else said.

I liked the way the ladies-in-waiting had little straps to slide their hands into as they carried that long train carefully behind Princess Elizabeth. I wondered how she felt as she walked down the aisle in Westminster Abbey to be crowned Queen, and I wished I were a princess, too.

"When can we have a television, Mam?" Joanne, Gillian and I chorused perpetually after we'd been to see Auntie Maggie's television set. We knew it was no use asking Dad. He'd just say, "Ask your mam."

But Mam just said, "When we can afford it," which was her answer to everything.

For months afterwards, I was obsessed. I drew Queen Elizabeth, coronets, tiaras and crowns, high-heeled shoes, long dresses, ladies in smart suits and wide hats. I traced the pictures from my Coronation book. My sisters were not nearly as impressed as I was with the pomp and circumstance of majesty.

The Coronation mugs, which came from the council, were taken off us as soon as we got them and stowed away in the display cabinet.

"In case they get broken. They'll be worth quite a bit in years to come, they will," my dad explained.

"I doubt it, seeing every child in Britain will be having one," my mam said dryly.

I asked Mam if she could help me make a train for my Elizabeth II, who had now metamorphosed from being baby Elizabeth. Mam found an old piece of red chenille and she sewed up the sides, threading a cord through the neck so Elizabeth could be a queen whenever I wanted her to be. I made her a cardboard crown covered with silver paper and a sceptre from a stick.

The Night Before Christmas

J. Winkley

But I still whispered special endearments, and if necessary administered punishment to Elizabeth when I decided she wasn't Queen Elizabeth II. She had to have a special time every day for getting some fresh air in her lungs, and was pushed out in her pram. I would sit her up, minus train and regalia, and walk her up and down our cobbled back street. So, she was both a baby and a queen — in fact, Elizabeth was everything to me.

WHEN Mrs Taylor, who looked after Standard II, asked if anyone had a doll that could be baby Jesus in the nativity play, I immediately put my hand up and volunteered baby Elizabeth.

I brought Elizabeth into school the next day, and every girl's head in the classroom craned as the teacher lifted the lid of the box and peered inside.

"She is beautiful, Clara. You are a lucky girl. But we'll have to wrap her in swaddling clothes so only her head shows — we don't want anyone to know we have a little girl as baby Jesus, do we?"

All the girls laughed, and chanted, "No, Mrs Taylor."

The boys showed no interest at all. They said they couldn't care less about sissy dollies.

The play did not pass off without incident. For the most part, the infants forgot their lines, and the prompter, who was my sister Joanne, was always late with her prompts. She was behind a curtain and could be heard in the

*THE night before
Christmas
Magic abounds,
Snow in the garden
In crystallised mounds,
Everything quiet
And put in its place,
And there on the table
A cloth made of lace.
The presents are wrapped
And in turn have been strung,
With socks for the children
Judiciously hung,
The tree in the corner
Has turned out its lights,
All is serene
On this night of all nights.
Then, in the morning,
The church bells will ring,
And time-honoured carols
We'll heartily sing,
You've never failed
To show us the way,
Many happy returns, Lord,
Of Your special day!*

— Brian H. Gent.

audience, she whispered so loudly. I could have died of embarrassment.

But baby Jesus saved the play. The spotlight was always on the crib, and the infants did look sweet in their home-made costumes. After the parents had left and a few of us had done the tidying, I went to the teacher, who gave me a special smile.

"Thank you for baby Jesus, Clara. Here she is. Be careful taking her home. She can be baby Elizabeth again now!"

"Thank you," I said proudly, putting him/her back into the cardboard box.

I could feel my sisters' irritation. The three of us walked home together. It wasn't far. Mam and Dad and Grandma and Grandad had gone ahead with the other parents.

"I saw you laughing at me," Joanne said.

"Well, you weren't exactly prompt at prompting, were you?" I said cheekily, clutching my shoebox.

Gillian started giggling, too.

"You were terrible. You've got the loudest whisper in Lancashire, Joanne." She was taunting her, running backwards in front of her.

Joanne lost her temper, and pushed Gillian. Then Joanne pushed me . . . hard . . . in the back. She pushed me so hard, and with such force, that I fell forwards, grazing my knees on the pavement.

But that didn't matter. What mattered was that the shoebox that had been in both my hands flew through the air in front of me. The lid had landed further up the street and Elizabeth was lying in a crumpled heap on her back near to her box.

The three of us stopped. Joanne just looked at my doll in stunned silence.

"I didn't mean to . . ." she stuttered.

"Well, you did . . ." Gillian said.

Tears were running down my face. I said nothing, just picked myself up, ignoring the blood running down my left leg. I went over to pick up the most precious doll in the world, now lying flat on her back on the wet, greasy pavement.

"Look at her, just look at her!" I sobbed.

Gillian silently took Elizabeth from me, and Joanne tried to wipe her down with her hankie. But Elizabeth's beautiful pink dress was muddy all down the back, her hair that had felt like feathers in my hands was now wet and filthy. Her kid shoes were scratched at the back and no longer white, and her white

171

silk stockings were dirty down one side.

"I knew you'd spoil her. Now you've finally done it." I grabbed my doll off Joanne and ran home, tore upstairs and threw myself on my bed. My chest was hurting, and my filthy doll was pressed against my best coat.

Mam rushed upstairs, followed moments later by Gillian and Joanne. By then I was sitting on the side of the bed hiccupping, feeling my heart was breaking.

"What's happened?"

Gillian and Joanne stood in silence. Would I tell on them?

"I fell over. There was a crack in the slabs, and the box fell out of my hands. Look at my dolly, Mam!" I cried.

Silently I passed Elizabeth over, my sisters' faces showing their relief. I'd not broken our golden rule of silence.

"Never mind, love." Mam was on her knees in front of me, cradling me in to her. "You're just a bit shocked. Get that dirty coat off. We'll wash those knees and put some iodine on them, then we'll see about Elizabeth.

"There are dolly hospitals if she's seriously injured, you know. But I don't think she is. I think she just needs washing," she said gently.

Tenderly, Mam took the doll from my tight grip. She looked suspiciously at my two sisters, who said nothing. She must have known something else had happened, but she never said a word, just took me off into the bathroom to wash my knee. She said she could brush the mud off my coat when it had dried.

I screeched when the iodine went on, but was pleased with the two enormous plasters on my knees.

"Now, let's go and see to little Elizabeth," Mam said.

We all trailed into my bedroom. There wasn't room for my sisters, but they stood in the doorway, both looking upset.

Carefully, Mam felt the back of her head.

"No fracture there," she said quietly. Then she felt all over Elizabeth's slight frame very carefully.

"No, nothing broken," she pronounced in a strong positive voice. I sat hopelessly on the bed, my face still red and swollen; my body slumped into itself. I still felt my world had come to an end.

"Come on, now, Clara, don't worry. She'll soon be as good as new," Mam said briskly. She lifted my chin and looked into my eyes and then smiled her special Mam smile, the one I always knew would make everything right.

And when Mam had finished, Elizabeth did look as good as new.

✳   ✳   ✳   ✳

The years go by, and everything changes. Now, Elizabeth is tired and out of date, a little bit grubby round the edges. She lives in a cupboard in her shoebox. Baby dolls are different now, with rubbery, lifelike faces, and they can drink milk from bottles and wet disposable nappies.

But, just sometimes, children find old things in cupboards that they fall in love with, and then history repeats itself. My granddaughter Elizabeth has taken to baby Elizabeth, and wants her to be in the nativity play at school. Of course, I was happy to oblige.

This time I'm a member of the audience. I manage to grab a seat at the end of the row, with my daughter Jane beside me.

The lights dim, and the curtains open. There is the traditional tableau with Mary and Joseph in the centre, everyone looking at baby Jesus. The spotlight shines once again on the crib. Mary is aged six, and Joseph seven. Joseph has his arm round Mary's shoulder.

The narrator, my little granddaughter, tells the simple tale of the first Christmas in between little songs. Tears fill my eyes.

It is so many years since Elizabeth's last appearance as baby Jesus, but it seems like yesterday. My daughter squeezes my hand. She understands; she has tears in her eyes, too.

Together we watch the play, listening to the young voices, some shy, some enjoying every minute. Children are so much more confident nowadays, aren't they?

MY hands hurt from all the clapping I do at the end. Eventually my granddaughter joins us.

I kiss her.

"A wonderful performance, Elizabeth. I've not enjoyed myself so much since last time."

"What do you mean, 'last time'?" Elizabeth asks, looking intrigued. She hands me the shoebox with elderly Elizabeth tucked up carefully inside.

"Oh, my dolly has acted the part of baby Jesus twice now. She's quite a star. She was in a nativity play when I was younger than you are now, Elizabeth."

"Well, she's brought us good luck tonight, Grandma. My teacher is ever so pleased with us."

"I'll bet she is — I'm proud of you, too," I tell her, giving her a big hug and a kiss.

Elizabeth the elderly dolly is stowed away in my shopping bag. Who knows? Somebody else might want to borrow her for another performance, one day. ■

Printed and Published in Great Britain by D.C. Thomson & Co., Ltd., Dundee, Glasgow and London.

ISBN 978 1 84535 355 1
EAN 9 781845 353551

Falkland Palace, Fife, Scotland

ALL my life I've loved reading about our past Kings and Queens. Mary, Queen of Scots was one of my particular favourites and when I read that she had often visited Falkland Palace, I was determined to go there, too.

My chance came when my husband had business in Edinburgh and we travelled up and then on to Falkland Palace for the day. The palace was everything that I thought it would be and took my breath away when I first set eyes on it. I could just imagine Mary, Queen of Scots and her entourage sweeping through the massive gatehouse and dismounting from their horses and carriages.

I loved the peaceful